A Country Christmas

Miss Read

* * * *

A COUNTRY CHRISTMAS

This omnibus first published in 2006 by Orion,
an imprint of the Orion Publishing Group Ltd,
Orion House, 5 Upper St Martin's Lane,
London, WC2H 9EA

1 3 5 7 9 10 8 6 4 2

A Country Christmas first published as part of the omnibus
entitled *Christmas at Fairacre* by Michael Joseph 1991
and Penguin Books 1992
Copyright © Miss Read 1991

Village Christmas first published by Michael Joseph 1966
Copyright © Miss Read 1966
Illustrations copyright © John S. Goodall 1966

The Fairacre Ghost and *Jingle Bells* from *Over the Gate*
first published by Michael Joseph 1964
Copyright © Miss Read 1964
Illustrations copyright © John S. Goodall 1964

Christmas at Caxley 1913 from *The Market Square*
first published by Michael Joseph 1966
Copyright Miss Read 1966
Illustrations copyright © John S. Goodall 1966

The White Robin first published by Michael Joseph 1979
Copright © Miss Read 1979
Illustrations copyright © John S. Goodall 1979

The following stories are taken from *Tales from a Village School*
first published by Michael Joseph 1994
Overall copyright © Miss Read 1994
Illustrations copyright © Kate Dicker 1994
Christmas Cards for Forty © *Punch* 1949;
The Craftsman © Miss Read 1954; *Carols for Forty* © *Punch* 1952;
Snow on Their Boots © Miss Read 1955;
Forty in the Wings © *Punch* 1951

The moral right of Miss Read to be identified as the author
of this work has been asserted in accordance with the Copyright,
Designs and Patents Act of 1988.

A CIP catalogue record for this book
is available from the British Library.

ISBN-13: 978 075287 384 8
ISBN-10: 0 7528 7384 9

Typeset at The Spartan Press Ltd, Lymington, Hants

Printed in Great Britain by Clays Ltd, St Ives plc

The Orion Publishing Group's policy is to use papers that
are natural, renewable and recyclable products and made
from wood grown in sustainable forests. The logging and
manufacturing processes are expected to conform to the
environmental regulations of the country of origin.

www.orionbooks.co.uk

Contents

* * * *

A COUNTRY CHRISTMAS

Foreword by Miss Read

I am delighted to see this winter collection from my writings about the imaginary village of Fairacre and its surroundings.

Winter may not be everyone's favourite season, but of all the year's festivals Christmas takes pride of place, and has lost none of its magic. This, no doubt, is partly because we hark back to the excitements of childhood Christmases but also because we look forward to renewing friendships and to taking part in the foremost of the church's festivals.

But the fact that Christmas Day falls in the dreariest time of the year also highlights its impact. We are usually in the grip of winter's cold, early darkness, frost and snow, and all the ills that they bring. Doubly precious, therefore, are our domestic comforts – a blazing fire, sustaining food, the comfort of friends and, at the end of the day, a warm bed.

In this collection of my writings about winter you will find many of these things. The celebrations and adventures mostly take place in the imaginary village of Fairacre, especially the school, the nearby market town of Caxley, or in that neighbourhood. Outside, the winter landscape has a beauty of its own: bare branches against a clear sky, brilliant stars on a frosty night and perhaps a swathe of untouched snow. But these beauties are best when seen from the comfort of one's home, with a good fire crackling and the smell of crumpets toasting for tea.

Although more than just the season of Christmas is covered in *The White Robin*, I am very pleased that this story has been included since it rather stood on its own and has not previously been in any of the Fairacre omnibuses.

That is the charm of the winter season, the contrast between the cold and the warmth, the light and the dark. I hope you will enjoy Christmas and the wintertime in the book before you.

Miss Read 1991

Village Christmas

Illustrated by J. S. Goodall

To Jill and John
with love

The darkness throbbed with the clamour of church bells. The six sonorous voices of St Patrick's peal chased each other, now in regular rhythm, now in staccato clashes, as the bell-ringers sweated at their Christmas peal practice.

The night was iron-cold. Frost glittered on the hedges and fields of Fairacre although it was not yet eight o'clock. Thatched roofs were furred with white rime beneath a sky brilliant with stars. Smoke rose in unwavering blue wisps from cottage chimneys, for the air was uncannily still.

The sound of the bells carried far in such weather. At Beech Green, three miles away, Miss Clare heard them clearly as she stooped to put her empty milk bottle tidily on her cottage doorstep, and she smiled at the cheerful sound. She knew at least four of those six bell-ringers for she had taught them their lessons long ago at Fairacre School. Arthur Coggs, furtively setting rabbit snares by a copse near Springbourne, heard them as clearly. The shepherd, high on the downs above the village, and the lonely signalman tending his oil-lamps on the branch line which meandered along the Cax valley to the market town, heard them too.

Nearer at hand, in the village of Fairacre, the bells caused more positive reactions. The rooks, roosting in the topmost boughs of the elm trees hard by the reverberating belfry, squawked an occasional protest at this disturbance. A fox, slinking towards Mr Willet's hen run, thought better of it as the bells rang out, and beat a retreat to the woods. Mrs Pringle, the dour cleaner of Fairacre School, picked up a flake of whitewash with disgust from the spotless floor where it had fluttered from the quaking kitchen wall, and a new baby nearby, awakened by the clamour, wailed its alarm.

Miss Margaret Waters and her sister Mary were quietly at work in their cottage in the village street. They sat, one each side of the big round table in the living room, penning their Christmas cards in meticulous copper plate. Music tinkled from the large old-fashioned wireless set on the dresser by

the fireplace, vying with the noise of the bells outside. Mary's grey curls began to nod in time to a
waltz, and putting her pen between her teeth, she
rose to increase the volume of the music. At that
moment an excruciating clashing of St Patrick's peal
informed the world of Fairacre that at least three of
the six bell-ringers were hopelessly awry in their
order.

'Switch it off, Mary, do! Them dratted bells
drowns anything else. We may as well save the
electric!' exclaimed Margaret, looking over the top
of her gold-rimmed spectacles.

Mary obeyed, as she always did, and returned to
her seat. It would have been very nice, she thought
privately, to hear 'The-Merry Widow' waltz all the
way through, but it was not worth upsetting Margaret – especially with Christmas so near. After all, it
was the season of goodwill. She picked up a card
from the central pile and surveyed it with affection.

'All right for Cousin Toby?' she queried, her head
on one side. 'He's partial to a robin.'

Her sister looked up from her writing and studied
the card earnestly. Sending just the right card to the
right person was something which both sisters con-
sidered with the utmost care. Their Christmas cards
had been chosen from the most modestly priced
counter at Bell's, the Caxley stationer's, but even so

the amount had been a considerable sum from the weekly pension of the two elderly sisters.

'You don't feel it's a mite spangly? That glitter on the icicles don't look exactly *manly* to me. I'd say the coach and horses myself.'

Mary set aside the robin reluctantly, and began to inscribe the card with the coach and horses:

From your affectionate cousins,
Margaret and Mary

The ancient mahogany clock, set four-square in the middle of the mantelpiece, ticked steadily as it had done throughout their parents' married life and their own single one. A log hissed on the small open fire, and the black kettle on the trivet began to hum. By bedtime it would be boiling, ready for the sisters' hot water bottles. It was very peaceful and warm in the cottage and Mary sighed with content as she tucked in the flap of Cousin Toby's envelope. It was the time of day she loved best, when the work was done, the curtains were drawn, and she and Margaret sat snugly and companionably by the fire.

'That seems to be the lot,' she observed, putting the envelopes into a neat stack. Margaret added her last one. Three, including the rejected robin, remained unused.

'There's bound to be someone we've forgot,' said Margaret. 'Put 'em all on the dresser, dear, and we'll post 'em off tomorrow.'

The church bells stopped abruptly and the room seemed very quiet. Ponderously and melodiously the old clock chimed half past eight from the mantel-piece, and Mary began to yawn. At that moment there came a sharp rapping at the door. Mary's mouth closed with a snap.

'Who on earth can that be, at this time of night?' she whispered. Her blue eyes were round with alarm. Margaret, made of sterner stuff, strode to the door and flung it open. There, blinking in the sudden light, stood a little girl.

'Come in, do, out of the cold,' begged Mary, who

had followed her sister. 'Why, Vanessa, you haven't got a coat on! You must be starved with the cold! Come by the fire now!'

The child advanced towards the blaze, plump hands outstretched like pink star-fish. She sniffed cheerfully and beamed up at the two sisters who looked down at her with so much concern. The child's two front milk teeth had recently vanished and the gap gave her wide smile a gamin air. She shook the silky fringe from her sparkling eyes. Clearly, Miss Vanessa Emery was very happy to be inside Flint Cottage.

'And what do you want, my dear, so late in the day?' enquired Margaret, unusually gentle.

'Mummy sent me,' explained the child. 'She said could you lend her some string to tie up Grandpa's parcel. *Thick* string, she said, if you could manage it. It's a box of apples, you see, off our tree, and sticky tape won't be strong enough on its own.'

'Indeed it won't,' agreed Mary opening the dresser drawer and taking out a square tin. She opened it and placed it on the table for the child to inspect. Inside were neat coils of string, the thickest at the left-hand side and the finest – some of it as thin as thread – in a tidy row on the right-hand. The child drew in her breath with delight and put a finger among the coils.

'Where did you buy it?' she asked.

'*Buy* it?' echoed Margaret, flabbergasted. 'Buy *string*? We've never bought a bit of string in all our borns! This comes off all the parcels that have come here over the years.'

'Mum cuts ours off and throws it away,' explained the child unabashed. She picked up a fat gingery coil of hairy twine and examined it closely.

'Could you spare this?' she asked politely.

'Of course, of course,' said Mary, hurrying to make amends for the horrified outburst from her sister. She tucked it into the pocket on the front of the child's cotton apron.

'And now I'll see you across the road,' she added, opening the front door. 'It's so late I expect you should be in bed.'

The child left the fire reluctantly. One hand gripped the string inside her pocket. The other she held out to Margaret.

'Good night, Miss Waters,' she said carefully, 'and thank you for the string.'

'You're welcome,' replied Margaret, shaking the cold hand. 'Mind the road now.'

The two sisters watched the child run across to the cottage opposite. It sat well back from the village street in a little hollow surrounded by an overgrown garden. Against the night sky its thatched roof and two chimneys gave it the air of a great cat crouched comfortably on its haunches. They heard the gate bang, and turned again to their fire, slamming the door against the bitter cold.

'Well!' exploded Margaret. 'Fancy sending a child out at this time of night! And for a bit of string! "Cuts it off" indeed! Did you ever hear of such a wicked waste, Mary?'

'Dreadful!' agreed her sister, but with less vehemence. 'And that poor little mite with no coat on!'

'Well, I've always said, there's some people as have no business to be parents and them Emerys belong to 'em. Three under seven and another on the way! It's far too many. I feel downright sorry for that poor unborn. She can't look after the three she's got already!'

Margaret picked up the poker and rapped smartly at a large lump of coal. It split obediently and burst into joyous flame. The kettle purred with increased vigour, and Margaret moved it further back on the trivet.

The two sisters sat down, one at each side of the blaze. From the cupboard under the dresser Mary drew forth a large bundle, unrolled it and gave one end to Margaret. They were making a hearthrug, a gigantic monster of Turkish design, in crimson and deep blue. Each evening the sisters spent some time thrusting their shining hooks in and out of the canvas as they laboriously added strand after strand of bright wool.

Margaret's end was growing much more quickly than Mary's. Her hook moved more briskly, with sharp staccato jabs, and the wool was tugged fiercely into place. Mary moved more slowly, and she fingered each knotted strand as though she loved it. She would be sorry when the work was finished. Margaret would be glad.

'I must say, they seem happy enough,' observed Mary, reverting to the topic of the Emerys. 'And very healthy too. They're dear little girls – and so polite. Did you notice the way Vanessa shook hands?'

'It's not the children I'm criticizing,' replied Margaret. 'It's their parents. There'll be four little mites under that roof soon, and dear knows how many more to come. And they don't seem to have any idea of bringing them up right! Look at their fancy names, for one thing! Vanessa, Francesca, Anna-Louise – I ask you!'

'I rather like them,' said Mary with spirit. Margaret snorted and jabbed the canvas energetically.

'And all dressed up in that frilly little apron with a heart-shaped pocket, and no decent warm coat on the child's back,' continued Margaret, now in full spate. 'It's all on a par with the house. All fancy lampshades, and knick-knacks hanging on the wall, and great holes in the sheets, for all to see, when she hangs 'em on the line. 'Twasn't no surprise to me to hear she cuts up her string and throws it out. We done right, Mary, not to get too familiar with her. She's the sort as would be in here, everlasting borrowing, given half a chance, as I told you at the outset.'

'I dare say you're right, dear,' responded Mary equably. She usually was, thought Mary, pensively. They worked in silence and Mary looked back to the time when the Emerys had first arrived in Fairacre, three months before, and she had watched from a vantage point behind the bedroom curtain their furniture being carried up the brick path.

It was a golden afternoon in late September and Margaret had gone to St Patrick's to help with the decorations for Harvest Festival. A bilious headache had kept Mary from accompanying her, and she had retired to bed with an aspirin and a cup of tea.

She had slept for an hour and the sound of children's voices woke her. At first she thought the school-children must be running home, but it was only three o'clock by the flowered china timepiece on the mantelshelf, and she had gone to the window to investigate.

A dark green pantechnicon almost blocked the

village street. The men were staggering to the house opposite with a large and shabby sideboard between them. Two little girls danced excitedly beside them, piping shrilly to each other like demented moorhens. Their mother, cigarette in mouth, watched the proceedings from the side of the doorway.

Mary was a little shocked – not by the cigarette, although she felt that smoking was not only a wicked waste of money but also very unhealthy – but at the young woman's attire. She wore black tights, with a good-sized hole in the left leg, and a short scarlet jerkin which ended at mid-thigh. Her black hair was long and straight, and her eyes were heavily made up. To Mary she appeared like an actress about to take part in a play set in the Middle

Ages. No one – absolutely no one – dressed like that in Fairacre, and Mary only hoped that the young woman would not hear the remarks which must inevitably come from such village stalwarts as Mrs Pringle and her own sister, if she continued to dress in this manner.

Nevertheless, Mary was glad to see that they had neighbours, and gladder still to see that there were children. The thatched cottage had stood empty all the summer, ever since the old couple who had lived there from the time of their marriage in good Queen Victoria's reign, had departed to a daughter's house in Caxley and had moved from thence to Fairacre churchyard. It would be good to see a light winking through the darkness again from the cottage window, and to see the neglected garden put into order once more, thought Mary.

Her headache had gone and she straightened the bed coverlet and made her way down the steep dark staircase. She was pleasantly excited by the activity outside the front door, and tried to hear what the children were saying, but in vain. A thin wailing could be heard and, peeping out from behind the curtain, Mary saw that the woman now had a baby slung over her shoulder and was patting its back vigorously.

'Three!' breathed Mary, with delight. She was

devoted to children and thoroughly enjoyed taking her Sunday School class. To be sure, she was often put out when some of the bigger boys were impudent, and was quite incapable of disciplining them, but small children, and particularly little girls of gentle upbringing, delighted her warm old spinster's heart.

When Margaret returned she told her the good news. Her sister received it with some reserve.

'I'll be as pleased as you are,' she assured Mary, 'if they behaves themselves. But let's pray they ain't the squalling sort. You can hear too much in that bedroom of ours when the wind's that way.'

'I wondered,' began Mary timidly, 'if it would be a kindness to ask 'em over for a cup of tea when we makes it.'

'If she was alone,' replied Margaret after a moment's consideration, 'I'd say "Yes" but with three children and the removal men too, I reckons we'd be overdone. Best leave it, Mary – but it does you credit to have thought of it.'

Mary was about to answer, but Margaret went on. Her expression was cautious.

'We don't want to be too welcoming yet awhile, my dear. Let's see how they turn out. Being neighbourly's one thing, but living in each other's pockets is another. Let 'em get settled and then we'll call.

Best not to go too fast or we'll find ourselves babysitting every evening.' A thought struck her. 'Seen the man, Mary?'

Mary admitted she had not.

'Funny!' ruminated her sister. 'You'd have thought he'd be on hand.'

'Maybe he's clearing things up the other end,' suggested Mary.

'Maybe,' agreed Margaret. 'I only hope and pray she's not a widow woman, or worse still one that's *been left*.'

'We'll soon know,' replied Mary comfortably, well versed in village ways. Fairacre had a lively grapevine, and there would be no secrets unhidden in the cottage opposite, the sisters felt quite sure.

Within a week it was common knowledge that the Emerys had moved from a north London suburb – Enfield, according to Mrs Pringle, Southgate, by Mr Willet's reckoning, though the Vicar was positive that it was Barnet. Much to Margaret's relief, Mr Emery had appeared, and her first glimpse of him was as he put out the milk bottles the next morning whilst still clad in dashing crimson pyjamas with yellow frogging.

He worked 'up the Atomic', as did many other

Fairacre residents, but drove there in a shabby old Daimler at about nine, instead of going on the bus which collected the other workers at seven-thirty each morning.

'One of the high-ups,' commented Mr Willet. 'Had a bit of book-learning in science and that, I don't doubt. Looks scruffy enough to have a degree, to my mind. Wants a new razor-blade, by the looks of things, and that duffle coat has seen a few meals down it.'

Fairacre was inclined to agree with Mr Willet's somewhat tart summing-up of Mr Emery, though the female residents pointed out that he seemed to take his share of looking after the children and, say what you like, he had very attractive thick black hair. It was Mrs Emery who provided more fodder for gossip.

As Mary had foreseen, her Bohemian garments scandalized the older generation. And then, she was so breathtakingly friendly! She had introduced herself to Mr Lamb in the Post Office, and to two venerable residents who were collecting their pensions, shaking hands with them warmly and asking such personal questions as where they lived and what were their names.

'Wonder she didn't ask us how old we be,' said one to the other when they escaped into the open air.

'She be a baggage, I'll lay. I'll take good care to steer clear of that 'un.'

She hailed everyone she met with equal heartiness, and struck horror into every conservative Fairacre heart by announcing her decision to join every possible club and society in the village 'to get to know people', and her intention of taking the little girls with her if the times of the meetings proved suitable.

'Terribly important for them to make friends,' she told customers and assistants in the village shop one morning. Her wide warm smile embraced them all. She seemed unaware of a certain frostiness in the air as she made her purchases, and bade them all goodbye, with considerable gusto, when she left.

Margaret and Mary viewed their ebullient neighbour with some alarm. Three days after her arrival, when Margaret was already planning the best time to call, Mrs Emery knocked briefly on the sisters' front door and almost immediately opened it herself.

'Anyone at home?' she chirped blithely. 'Can I come in?'

Before the startled sisters could reply, she was in the room, with two beaming little girls following her.

'I'm your new neighbour, as I expect you know,' she said, smiling disarmingly. 'Diana Emery. This is

Vanessa, and this one Francesca. Say "Hello", dar-
lings.'

'Hello!' 'Hello!' piped the two children.

Mary collected her wits with remarkable com-
posure. She found the Emery family attractive,
despite their forward ways.

'There now!' she began kindly. 'We were wondering when to call and see you. Won't you take a cup
of coffee? Margaret and I usually have some about
this time.'

'I'll get it,' said Margaret swiftly, glad to escape
for a moment to take stock of the situation. Mary
could see from her expression that she was not
pleased by the invasion.

'Lovely!' sighed Mrs Emery, flinging off a loose
jacket of jade green, and settling in Margaret's armchair. The two little girls collapsed cross-legged on
the hearth-rug and gazed about them with squirrel-
bright eyes beneath their silky fringes.

'What about the baby?' asked Mary, concerned
lest it should have been left outside. The morning
was chilly.

'Not due until the New Year,' replied Mrs Emery
nonchalantly. 'And jolly glad I shall be when it's
arrived.'

There was a gasp from the doorway as Margaret
bore in the tray. She was pink, and obviously put out.

Mary hastened to explain. 'I meant the *third* little girl,' she said.

'Oh, Anna-Louise! She's fast asleep in the pram. Quite safe, I can assure you.'

'We want a brother next time,' announced Vanessa, eyeing the plate of biscuits.

'Three girlth ith three too many,' announced Francesca. 'Thatth's what my daddy thayth.'

'That's a joke,' explained Vanessa.

'Sometimes I wonder,' their mother said, but her tone was cheerful.

Margaret poured coffee and tried to avert her eyes from Mrs Emery's striped frock which gaped widely at the waist fastening, displaying an extraordinary undergarment of scarlet silk. Could it *possibly* be a petticoat, Margaret wondered? Were there really petticoats in existence of such a remarkable colour?

Mary did her best to make small talk. It was quite apparent that Margaret was suffering from shock, and was of little help.

'Is there anything you want to know about the village? Perhaps you go to church sometimes? The services are ten-thirty and six-thirty.'

'We're not much good at church-going,' admitted their neighbour. 'Though I must say the Vicar looks a perfect poppet.'

Margaret swallowed a mouthful of coffee too

quickly and coughed noisily. This was downright sacrilege.

'Gone down the wrong way,' explained Francesca, coming close to her and gazing up anxiously into Margaret's scarlet face. Speechless, but touched by the child's solicitude, Margaret nodded.

'And if you want to go to Caxley,' continued Mary, 'there is a bus timetable on the wall of The Beetle and Wedge. Is there anything else we can help you with?'

Mrs Emery put her cup carelessly upon its saucer so that the spoon crashed to the floor. Both children pounced upon it and returned it to the table.

'Well, yes, there is something,' said their mother. 'Could you possibly change a cheque for me? I'm absolutely out of money and want to get some cigarettes. Edgar won't be home until eight or after.'

There was a chilly silence. The sisters had no banking account, and the idea of lending money, even to their nearest and dearest, was against their principles. To be asked, by a stranger, to advance money was profoundly shocking. Margaret found her tongue suddenly.

'I'm afraid we can't oblige. We keep very little in the house. I suggest that you ask Mr Lamb. He may be able to help.' Her tone was glacial, but Mrs Emery appeared unperturbed.

'Ah well,' she said cheerfully, struggling from the armchair and gaping even more hugely at the waist band, 'never mind! I'll try Mr Lamb, as you suggest. Must have a cigarette now and again with this brood to look after.'

She picked up the green jacket and smiled warmly upon the sisters.

'Thank you so much for the delicious coffee. Do pop over and see us whenever you like. We'll probably be seeing quite a bit of each other as we're such close neighbours.'

And with these ominous words she made her departure.

*

Ever since then, thought Mary, busily prodding her hook in the rug, she and Margaret had fought a polite, but quietly desperate, battle against invasion.

'Be friendly to all, but familiar with few,' said an old Victorian sampler hanging on their cottage wall. The sisters found its advice timely. The children, they agreed, were adorable, and although they appeared far too often for 'a-shilling-for-the-electricity-meter' or 'a-box-of-matches-because-the-shop's-shut' and other like errands, the two sisters had not the heart to be annoyed with them. In any case, it was simple to dismiss them when their business was done, with a piece of chocolate to sweeten their departure.

Mrs Emery, growing weekly more bulky, was more difficult to manage, and the two sisters grew adept at making excuses. Once inside, she was apt to stay over an hour, seriously throwing out the working of the sisters' day. She certainly was an embarrassment as a neighbour.

Mary's eyes strayed to the table, and the rejected Christmas card with the gay robin among his spangles. A thought struck her, and she put down her hook.

'Margaret,' she said suddenly, 'what about sending that robin to the Emery children?'

Margaret began to look doubtful.

'Well, my dear, you know what a mite of trouble we've had with that woman! I just wonder—'

'Oh, do now!' pressed Mary, her face flushed. ''Tis Christmas! No time for hard thoughts, sister, and them children would just love it. I could slip over with it after dark on Christmas Eve and pop it through the letter box.'

Margaret's face relaxed into a smile.

'We'll do it, Mary, that we will!'

She began to roll up the rug briskly, as the church clock struck ten. Mary gave a happy sigh, and lifted the singing kettle from the trivet.

'Time for bed,' she said, taking two hot water bottles from the bottom of the dresser cupboard.

'Think of it, Margaret! Only three more days until Christmas!'

The next three days were busy ones for the ladies at Flint Cottage. Red-berried holly, pale mistletoe and glossy ivy were collected, and used to decorate the living room. Two red candles stood one at each end of the mantelpiece, and a holly garland hung from the brass knocker on the front door.

The cake was iced, the pudding fetched down from the top shelf in the pantry, the mincemeat jar stood ready for the pies and a trifle was made. One of Mrs Pringle's chickens arrived ready for the table, and sausage meat came from the butcher.

Margaret crept away privately while Mary was bringing in logs from the woodshed, and wrapped up two pairs of sensible lisle stockings which she had bought in Caxley for her sister's present. Mary took advantage of Margaret's absence at the Post Office and swiftly wrapped up a pair of stout leather gloves and hid them in the second drawer of the bedroom chest.

All Fairacre was abustle. Margaret and Mary helped to set up the Christmas crib in the chancel of St Patrick's church. The figures of Joseph, Mary and the Child, the shepherds and the wise men reappeared every year, standing in the straw provided by Mr Roberts the farmer, and lit with sombre beauty by discreetly placed electric lights. The children came in on their way from school to see this perennial scene, and never tired of looking.

The sisters helped to decorate the church too. There were Christmas roses on the altar, their pearly beauty set off by sprigs of dark yew amidst the gleaming silverware.

On Christmas Eve the carol singers set out on their annual pilgrimage round the village. Mr Annett, the choir master, was in charge of the church choir and any other willing chorister who volunteered to join the party. This year, the newcomer Mr Emery was among them, for word had soon got round that he sang well and Mr Annett had invited him to join the carol singers. Clad in the duffle coat which Mr Willett thought of so poorly, he strode cheerfully along the frosty lanes of Fairacre, swinging a hurricane lamp as though he had lived in the village all his life, and rattling away to his companions with the same friendly foreign loquacity as his wife's.

One of their stopping places was outside The Beetle and Wedge, strategically placed in the village street. Margaret and Mary opened their window and watched the singers at their work. Their breath

rose in silver clouds in the light of the lanterns. The white music sheets fluttered in the icy wind which spoke of future snow to the weather-wise of Fairacre. Some of the lamps were hung on tall stout ashsticks, and these swayed above the ruffled hair of the men and the hooded heads of the women.

Mr Annett conducted vigorously and the singing was controlled as well as robust. As the country voices carolled the eternal story of joyous birth, Mary felt that she had never been so happy. Across the road she could see the upstairs light in the bed-room of the Emery children, and against the glowing pane were silhouetted two dark heads.

How excited they must be, thought Mary! The stockings would be hanging limply over the bed rail, just as her own and Margaret's used to hang so many years ago. There was nothing to touch the exquisite anticipation of Christmas Eve.

> *'Hark the herald angels sing,*
> *Glory to the new-born King,'*

fluted the choir boys, their eyes on Mr Annett, their mouths like dark Os in the lamplight. And the sound of their singing rose like incense to the thousands of stars above.

On Christmas morning Margaret and Mary were up early and went to eight o'clock service. A feeling of night still hung about the quiet village, although the sun was staining the eastern sky and giving promise of a fine day ahead.

The lighted crib glowed in the shadowy chancel like the star of Bethlehem itself, and the aromatic smell of the evergreens added to the spirit of Christmas. Later, the bells would ring out and the winter sunshine would touch the flowers and silver on the altar with brightness. All would be glory and rejoicing, but there was something particularly lovely and holy about these quiet early morning devotions, and the two sisters preferred to attend then, knowing that the rest of the morning would be taken up with the cheerful ritual of Christmas Day cooking.

They unwrapped their few parcels after breakfast, exclaiming with genuine pleasure at the modest calendars and handkerchiefs, the unaccustomed luxury of richly perfumed soap or chocolates which friends and relatives had sent.

Margaret thanked Mary warmly for the gloves. Mary was equally delighted with her stockings. They exchanged rare kisses and told each other how lucky they were.

'There's not many,' said Margaret, 'as can say they live as contented as we do here. And under our own roof, thank God, and nothing owing to any man!'

'We've a lot to be thankful for,' agreed Mary, folding up the bright wrappings neatly. 'Best of all each other – and next best, our health and strength, sister.'

'Now, I'm off to stuff the bird,' announced Margaret, rising with energy. 'I'll put on the pudding too while I'm in the kitchen. Must have that properly hotted up by midday.'

She bustled off and Mary began to make up the fire, and sweep the hearth. The two red candles looked brave and gay, standing like sentinels each side of the Christmas cards ranged along the mantelpiece. She wondered if the Emery children had liked the fat robin. She could see them now, in imagination, surrounded by new Christmas presents, flushed and excited at the joy of receiving and of giving.

At that moment, a rapping came at the front door and she rose from her sweeping to open it. Vanessa stood there, looking far from flushed and excited.

The child's eyes were large with alarm, her face pale with cold and fright.

'What is it, my love? Come in quickly,' cried Mary.

'It's Mummy. She said, "Could you come over, please?" She's ill.'

'Is Daddy with her?' asked Margaret, appearing in the doorway with her fingers pink and sticky with sausage meat.

'No. He's had to go to Grandma's. Grandpa rang up last night after we'd gone to bed. Grandma's being stroked.'

'Had a stroke,' corrected Margaret automatically. 'Dear me, that's bad news! We'll be over as soon as we've put the dinner in.'

The child's eyes grew more enormous than ever. She looked imploringly at Mary.

'But it's the baby coming! You must come this minute. Please, *please*!'

Without a word Margaret began to take off her kitchen apron.

'Go over, Mary,' she said quietly. 'I'll follow you.'

Indescribable chaos greeted Mary's eyes when she stepped into the Emery's kitchen. It was a large square room with a brick floor, and comfortably warmed by an Esse cooker appallingly streaked with grime. Quantities of anthracite dust were

31

plentifully sprinkled on the floor at its base, and had been liberally trodden about the room.

The débris of breakfast littered the table, and coloured paper, tags and string garnished sticky cereal bowls and mugs. A ginger cat lapped up some milk which dripped from an overturned jug, and the confusion was made more acute by Francesca who stood proudly holding a new scarlet scooter, ringing the shiny bell without cessation.

'Give over, do!' begged Mary, peremptory in her flurry. The child obeyed, still beaming. Nothing could quench her Christmas bliss, and Mary was immediately glad to see that this was so. The sound of Anna-Louise's wailing became apparent, and Mary opened the door of the box staircase and began to mount. The two little girls started to follow her.

'You stop here, there's dears,' said Mary, much agitated. Who knows what terrors might be aloft? 'Pick up the paper and make it nice and tidy.'

To her relief they fell upon the muddle joyously, and she creaked her way above. Mrs Emery's voice greeted her. She sounded as boisterous as ever, and Mary's fears grew less. At least she was conscious!

'You are a darling! You really are!' cried Mrs Emery. She was standing by the window, a vast figure in a red satin dressing gown embroidered on the back with a fierce dragon. Mary suddenly realized how very young she looked, and her heart went out to her.

'We were so sorry to hear about your mother-in-law,' began Mary, a little primly.

'Poor sweet,' said Mrs Emery. 'It *would* have to happen now. Edgar went off as soon as he came back from carol-singing. And then, this! *Much* too early. I suppose I've got the dates wrong again. Ah well!'

She sighed, and suddenly clutched the front of her dressing gown again. Mary felt panic rising.

'Do get into bed there's a love,' she begged, turning back the rumpled bedclothes invitingly. The bottom sheet had a tear in it six inches long, and a very dirty rag doll with the stuffing coming out. Mary was appalled. She must put something clean on the bed! Suppose the baby was born in that unhygienic spot! She looked for help towards Mrs Emery, who was bowed before the chest of drawers and gasping in an alarming way.

'You must have clean sheets,' announced Mary with an authoritative ring in her voice which wholly surprised her.

'Cupboard,' gasped Mrs Emery, nodding towards the next room.

An unpleasant smell was the first thing that Mary noticed about the adjoining bedroom. Anna-Louise was standing in a cot. Her nightgown and the bedding were ominously stained, but her cries had ceased and she threw Mary a ravishing smile.

'You pretty thing!' cried Mary, quite entranced. 'Aunt Mary'll see to you in just a minute.'

She swiftly ransacked the cupboard. She found a roll of mackintosh sheeting and two clean linen ones. Bustling back to the bedroom she set about making the bed with vigorous speed. Mrs Emery was upright again, leaning her damp forehead against the cool window-pane. She consented to be led to the bed, unprotesting, and let Mary remove the flamboyant dressing gown.

'There, there!' soothed Mary, tucking her in as though she were a child. 'I'll bring you a drink.'

'I'm all right now,' whispered the girl, and at that moment Margaret appeared.

'Does Nurse know?' was her first remark. Mary felt suddenly guilty. Of course, it was the first thing she should have found out. Trust Margaret to know exactly what to do!

'Yes,' replied Mrs Emery. 'At least, someone at her house does. Nurse was out on another baby case. They were sending word.'

'What about Doctor Martin?' continued Margaret.

'Nurse will get him, if need be,' said the girl. She

sank back on the pillow and suddenly looked deathly tired. 'It won't come for hours,' she told them. 'It's just that I was worried about the children.'

'I know, I know,' said Margaret gently. 'We'll look after them all right. Leave it all to us.'

'Anna-Louise needs a wash,' said Mary, retiring to the next room. She beckoned Margaret to follow her, and closed the door between the two rooms.

'What on earth shall we do?' she implored Margaret. Margaret, for once, looked flummoxed.

'Dear knows, and that's the honest truth,' admitted her sister. 'Let's hope nature knows best and Nurse comes pretty smartly. This is foreign stuff to us, Mary, but we must hold the fort till help comes.'

She turned to survey Anna-Louise who was jumping rhythmically up and down in the cot, with dire results.

'Land's sake, Mary! That child wants dumping in the bath – and the bedding too!'

'I'll do her,' said Mary swiftly. 'And then I can keep an eye on Mrs Emery up here. You see to things downstairs.'

'Won't do no harm to give Nurse another ring,' observed Margaret, turning to the door. She looked back at her sister. 'Who'd a thought we'd a been spending Christmas like this?'

She vanished downstairs and Mary went to turn on the bath for her charge.

Anna-Louise, well-soaped, was absolutely adorable. Fat and pink, with a skin like satin, she made Mary a willing slave. She patted the water vigorously, sending up showers of spray, and drenching Mary kneeling beside the bath. Mary could have stayed there all day, murmuring endearments and righting the celluloid duck time and time again. But the water cooled rapidly, and there was much to do. She gathered the naked child into a grubby bath towel, and dried her on her lap.

'She hasn't had her breakfast yet,' Mrs Emery said

drowsily when the child was dressed. She looked at her daughter with amusement. 'That's Francesca's jumper,' she observed, 'but no matter. Tie a bib on the poor lamb. She's a filthy feeder.'

Below stairs, all was amazingly quiet. The table had been cleared and the two little girls were blissfully engaged in filling in their new Christmas drawing books with glossy long crayons as yet unbroken. Margaret was busy sweeping the floor with a broom from which most of the bristles had long vanished.

'Has the baby come yet?' asked Vanessa, without looking up from the mad oscillation of her crayoning.

'Not yet,' replied Mary, threading Anna-Louise's fat legs through her high-chair. She stood back and surveyed the baby anxiously, 'And what does Anna-Louise like for breakfast?'

Francesca put down her crayon and gazed earnestly at her younger sister. 'She liketh bacon rindth betht,' she told Mary.

'Well, we've no time to cook bacon,' said Margaret flatly, still wielding the broom.

'Egg,' said Vanessa briefly. 'All horrible and runny. That's what she likes.'

The sisters exchanged questioning glances.

'Sounds reasonable,' muttered Margaret, 'if you can find the egg saucepan.'

'It's the milk one as well,' volunteered Vanessa, making for a cupboard. 'Here you are.' She produced a battered saucepan with a wobbly handle, and returned to the drawing book.

'Did you get through to Nurse?' asked Mary agitatedly, as she filled the saucepan.

'Still out. Message supposed to have been passed on. I reckons we ought to get her husband back. It's his business after all.' Margaret spoke with some asperity.

'I'll go and ask Mrs Emery,' said Mary, 'while the egg boils.'

She returned to the bedroom to find Mrs Emery humped under the bedclothes with her head in the pillow. She was groaning with such awful intensity that Mary's first impulse was to fly for Margaret, but she controlled it. She patted the humped back consolingly and waited for the spasm to pass. Somewhere, far away it seemed, the bells of St Patrick's began to peal for morning service. A vivid picture of the peaceful nave, the holly and the Christmas roses, the fragrance of the cypress and yew, came clearly to Mary, standing helplessly there watching her neighbour in labour. How long ago, it seemed, since she and Margaret knelt in the church! Yet only three hours had gone by.

The spasm passed and Diana Emery's face appeared again.

'Better,' she said. 'Can I have that drink now? Coffee, please – no milk. Any sign of that confounded nurse?'

'She's on her way,' said Mary, 'And we thought we ought to phone your husband.'

'His parents aren't on the telephone,' said Mrs Emery.

'We could ring the police,' suggested Mary with sudden inspiration.

Mrs Emery laughed with such unaffected gaiety that Mary could hardly believe that she had so recently been in such pain.

'It's not *that* serious. Nurse will be along any

minute now, and think how wonderful it will be to present Edgar with a fine new baby!'

She sounded so matter-of-fact and cheerful that Mary gazed at her open-mouthed. Was childbearing really undertaken so lightly? She remembered Margaret's tart comments on people who had large families with such apparent fecklessness. How many more would there be in this casual household, Mary wondered? Then she remembered the sight of Anna-Louise in the bath and hoped suddenly, and irrationally, that there would be more – lots more – and that she would be able to enjoy them.

'I'll get your coffee, my love,' she said warmly and went below.

Returning with the steaming black brew, she remembered something. 'Shouldn't we put the baby's things ready for Nurse?' she asked.

'There's not a great deal,' confessed the girl, warming her hands round the cup. 'I intended to do most of the shopping after Christmas in Caxley. So many people about, I just couldn't face it.'

'But you must have *some* things,' persisted Mary aghast.

'In the bottom drawer,' said the girl vaguely. 'And there are lots of Anna-Louise's things that will do, in the airing cupboard.'

Mary was shocked at such a slapdash approach to

an important event, and her face must have shown it, for Mrs Emery laughed.

'After the first you don't bother quite so much,' she confessed. 'You can get by with all the odds and ends the others had.'

Mary found six new nappies in the drawer, and a bundle of small vests, some tiny night-gowns yellow with much washing, and a shawl or two, in the airing cupboard.

'And what shall we put the baby in?' she inquired.

'Anna-Louise's carry-cot. It's in her room. It probably wants clean things in it.' The girl had slipped down into the bed again and closed her eyes. She looked desperately tired, thought Mary, with a pang.

The carry-cot held two dolls, a headless teddy-bear and a shoe, all carefully tucked up in a checked tablecloth. Mary took it downstairs to wash it out and dry it ready for the new occupant.

'If that dratted nurse don't come soon,' said Margaret, 'I'll fetch Doctor Martin myself, that I will! I'll just slip over home, Mary, and turn that bird and add a mite of hot water to the pudding.'

'We'll never have a chance to eat dinner, sister,' cried Mary. 'Not as things are!'

'There's them three to think of,' replied Margaret nodding to the children. 'We've got them to feed, don't forget.'

She lifted the latch and hurried across to their cottage. One or two parishioners, in their Sunday best, were making their way to church. Mary saw Mr and Mrs Willet stop to speak to her sister as she stood with one hand on the door knob. There was much headshaking, and Mrs Willet looked across at the Emerys' house with some alarm.

'The news will soon be round Fairacre,' thought Mary, as she dried the carry-cot.

It was clean and peaceful now in the kitchen, and she noticed the paper chains festooned against the ceiling, and the Christmas cards pinned along the rafters. Her own fat robin was there, and she glowed with pleasure. Vanessa and Francesca were still engrossed in their artistic efforts, and Anna-Louise wiped her eggy plate with her fingers and sucked them happily. What dear good children they were, thought Mary!

At that moment she heard their mother calling from overhead. Her voice sounded shrill and desperate. Mary took the stairs at a run. The girl was sitting up in bed, clenching and unclenching her hands on the coverlet.

'You *must* get that nurse – or the doctor, or someone. I can't stick this now. It's coming pretty fast.'

'I'll ring again,' promised Mary, thoroughly frightened by the urgency of the girl's pleas. 'Just lie down again. I'm sure it's better. Can I do anything? Rub your back, say, or bring you a hot bottle?'

She did her best to appear calm, but inwardly terror gripped her. Supposing the baby came this minute? What on earth did you do with a new-born baby? Wasn't there something about cutting a cord? And if so, where did you cut it? And how did you tie it up afterwards? Hadn't she heard once that mothers bled to death if the cord wasn't tied properly? And that wretched carry-cot wouldn't be anywhere near aired, let along made up with clean bedding, if the baby arrived now! Mary found herself shaking with panic, and praying desperately.

Don't let it come yet, please, dear Lord! Not until Nurse arrives, please God!

'There, my love—' she began, when she stopped abruptly. The door of the staircase had opened and someone was mounting.

'Margaret!' she cried. 'Quickly, Margaret!'

A sturdy figure appeared in the doorway.

'Nurse! Thank God!' cried Mary, and began to weep.

'You go and make us all a cup of tea,' said Nurse Thomas with gruff kindness. And Mary fled.

An hour later, Margaret and Mary sat at their own table, serving three excited little girls with Christmas dinner. Nurse's car still stood outside the cottage opposite, but Doctor Martin's was not to be seen. Evidently all was going well, and Nurse had everything well in hand.

Mary found herself as excited as the children. What a relief it was to be home again, and to know that Mrs Emery was being properly nursed! It was impossible to eat amidst such momentous happenings, and she was glad to neglect her own plate and to have the pleasant task of guiding Anna-Louise's teaspoon in the right direction.

St Patrick's clock chimed three, and still no message came from the house across the road.

A few Fairacre folk began to go by, taking an afternoon stroll for the sake of their digestions, between Christmas dinner and the further challenge of iced cake for tea. They noted Nurse's car and the light in the upstairs window, and fell to wondering.

Margaret was reading *The Tale of Two Bad Mice* from a new glossy copy which the children had received that morning, when a tapping came at the door. Mrs Lamb from the Post Office stood outside with a posy of anemones in her hand. She caught sight of the little girls inside and spoke in a whisper.

'For their mother, my dear. Hope all's going well. We heard about it after church. You're going over again, I expect?'

'Yes indeed,' answered Margaret, accepting the bright bunch. 'She'll be pleased with these. Nurse is still there, as you see.' She nodded towards the car.

'Give Mrs Emery our best wishes,' said Mrs Lamb. 'Poor soul, without her husband too! She's got everyone's sympathy, that's a fact.'

She set off homeward, and Margaret returned to the fireside. It began to grow dark, for the afternoon was overcast, and Mary took a taper and lit the bright red candles. The flames stretched and dwindled in the draught and the little girls gazed at them starry-eyed.

'Do you always have candles?' asked Vanessa. 'Or just at Christmas?'

'Just at Christmas,' said Margaret.

She put down the book and gazed at the bright flames with the children. The waiting seemed endless, and suddenly she felt desperately tired. How much longer, she wondered, before they knew?

Just then they heard the sound of a gate shutting and footsteps coming to their door. The two eldest sisters exchanged swift glances. Could it be –?

Mary opened the door and there stood the nurse, smiling.

'Come in,' said Mary.

'I daren't. I'm late now,' said Nurse, 'but all's well.'

Margaret and the children gathered at the door.

'A boy,' Nurse announced proudly. 'Seven pounds and bonny. And Mrs Emery's asleep. Can one of you go over?'

'You go,' said Margaret to Mary. 'I'll bring the children over later.'

'We want to see him,' pleaded Vanessa.

'*Now!*' added Francesca stubbornly.

'Now!' echoed Anna-Louise, not understanding the situation, but glad to try a new word.

'Later on,' responded Nurse firmly. 'Your mummy's tired.'

She turned to go and then looked back. 'Mr Emery rang up. I've told him the news and he'll be back very soon.'

She waved and made her way across the road to the car. 'Tell Mr Emery I'll be in, in the morning,' she called, and drove off in a cloud of smoke.

As if by magic, two heads popped out from the doorway of The Beetle and Wedge. They belonged to the landlord and his wife.

'Couldn't help seeing Nurse go off,' he said to Mary. 'What is it?'

'A boy!' said Mary, smiling.

'Now, ain't that good news?' beamed his wife. 'You tell her we'll be wetting the baby's head in here tonight.'

'Ah, she's a grand little mother, for all her funny ways,' declared her husband. 'Tell her it'll be nice to have another young 'un in the village.'

Mary tiptoed into the silent cottage. Everything seemed to slumber. The cat slept on a chair by the stove. Nothing moved.

She left the door of the staircase ajar so that she could hear the slightest sound from above, and sat down at the table.

In the domestic stillness which enveloped her, after the stress of the day, old and lovely words came into her mind.

'And it came to pass, while they were there, the days were fulfilled that she should be delivered.

'And she brought forth her first-born son; and she wrapped him in swaddling clothes, and laid him in a manger, because there was no room for them in the inn.'

Mary sat motionless, savouring the age-old miracle of the Nativity. And here, in this house, was another Christmas baby! She felt that she could not wait another moment. She must see him.

She slipped off her stout country shoes and tiptoed up the stairs. It was very quiet in the bedroom. Mrs Emery, looking pathetically young and pale, slept deeply. Beside the bed, on two chairs, was the carry-cot.

Mary leant over and gazed in wonder. Swaddled tightly, in the shawl she had found for him in the airing cupboard, was the new-born baby, as oblivious of the world about him as his sleeping mother.

Mary's heart beat with such fervour that she wondered that the sleepers did not wake. Full of joy, she crept below once more, and in her dizzy head beat the words:

'And the angel said unto them, Be not afraid; for behold, I bring you good tidings of great joy which shall be to all people.'

There was a sound outside, and she looked up from lacing her shoes. There stood Mr Emery, his face alight.

'Where is she?' he asked.

'They're both upstairs,' whispered Mary, and opened the staircase door so that he could go aloft and see his son.

Late that night, the two sisters sat each side of the hearth, working at their rug.

'D'you know what Vanessa said when her father fetched her?' asked Margaret. 'She said: "This is the loveliest Christmas we've ever had!" 'Twas good of the child to say it, I thought, after such a muddling old day. It touched me very much.'

'She spoke the truth,' replied Mary slowly. 'Not only for herself, but for all of us here in Fairacre. 'Tis a funny thing, sister, but when I crept up the stairs to take a first look at that new babe, the thought came to me: "Ah! You're a true Fairacre child, just as I was once, born here, and most likely to be bred up here, the Lord willing!" And then another thought came: "You've warmed up us cold old Fairacre folk

quicker'n the sun melts frost." You know, Margaret,
them Emerys have put us all to shame, many a
time, with their friendly ways, and been snubbed
too, often as not. It took a Christmas baby to kindle
some proper Christmas goodwill in Fairacre.'

''Tis true,' admitted Margaret, putting down the
rug hook, and gazing into the dying fire. Into her
tired mind there floated irrelevant memories . . . Mrs
Emery's scarlet petticoat, a ginger cat lapping milk,
Anna-Louise fumbling with her egg-spoon, while her
sisters watched her with squirrel-bright eyes, laugh-
ing at her antics . . . all adding up to colour and
warmth and gentle loving-kindness.

'Now this has happened,' she said soberly, 'it
won't stop at *Christmas* goodwill, sister. The Emerys

are part and parcel of this village for good. There's room for all sorts in Fairacre, Mary, but it took a newborn babe to show us.'

She began to roll up the rug briskly.

'Come, sister. Time we was abed.'

The Fairacre Ghost

Illustrated by J. S. Goodall

The Easter holidays are probably more welcome than any other, for they mark the passing of the darkest and most dismal of the three school terms and they herald the arrival of flowers, sunshine and all the pleasures of the summer.

At this time, in Fairacre, we set about our gardens with zeal. Potatoes are put in, on Good Friday if possible, and rows of peas and carrots, and those who have been far-sighted enough to put in their broad beans in the autumn, go carefully along the rows, congratulating themselves, and hoping that the black fly will not devastate the young hopefuls in the next few months.

We admire each other's daffodils, walk down each

other's garden paths observing the new growth in herbaceous borders, and gloat over the buds on plum and peach trees. We also observe the strong upthrust of nettles, couch grass and dandelions, among the choicer growth, but are too besotted by the thought of summer ahead to let such things worry us unduly.

It is now that the vicar gets out his garden furniture – a motley collection ranging from Victorian ironwork to pre-war Lloyd-loom – and arranges it hopefully on the vicarage veranda. Now Mr Mawne, our local ornithologist, erects a hide at the end of his lovely garden in order to watch the birds. He weaves a bower of peasticks, ivy-trails and twigs upon the wood and sacking framework, as intricate as the nests of those he watches.

Now the cottage doors are propped open with a chair, or a large stone, and striped cats wash their ears or survey the sunshine blandly through half-closed eyes. Tortoises emerge, shaky and slower than ever, from their hibernation, and sometimes a grass snake can be seen sunning itself in the dry grass.

This is the time for visiting and being visited. For months we have been confined. Bad weather, dirty roads, dark nights and winter illnesses have kept

us all apart. Now we set about refurbishing our friendships, and one of my first pleasures during this Easter holiday was a visit from my godson Malcolm Annett, and his father and mother.

It was a perfect day for a tea party. The table bore a bowl of freshly-picked primroses, some lemon curd made that morning, and a plentiful supply of egg sandwiches. Mr Roberts, the farmer, has a new batch of Rhode Island Red hens who supply me with a dozen dark brown eggs weekly. These are lucky hens, let me say, garrulous and energetic, running at large in the farmyard behind the house, scratching busily in the loose straw at the foot of the ricks, and advancing briskly to the back door whenever anyone emerges holding a plate. No wonder that their eggs are luscious compared with the product of their poor imprisoned sisters.

After tea we ambled through the village, greeting many old friends who were out enjoying the air. Mrs Annett used to teach at Fairacre before she married the headmaster at our neighbouring village Beech Green so that she knows a great many families here. Mr Annett is choirmaster at St Patrick's church at Fairacre, so that he too knows us all well.

We walked by the church and took a fork to the left. It is a lane used little these days, except by young lovers and Mr Roberts' tractors making their way to one of his larger fields. A dilapidated cottage stands alone some hundred yards from the entrance to the lane.

We stopped at its rickety gate and surveyed the outline of its ancient garden. A damson tree, its trunk riven with age, leant towards the remaining patch of roof thatch. Rough grass covered what once had been garden beds and paths, and nettles and brambles grew waist high against the walls of the ruin.

The doors and windows gaped open. Inside, on the ground floor, in what had once been the living room of the cottage, we could see hundredweight paper bags of fertilizer propped against the stained and ragged wallpaper. They belonged to Mr Roberts and were waiting to be spread upon his meadows any day now. Upstairs, the two small bedrooms lay open to the sky. The thatch had retreated before the onslaught of wind and weather, and only the frame of the roof stood, gaunt and rotting, against the evening sky.

'It must have been pretty once,' I said, looking at the triangle of garden and the rose-red of the old bricks.

'The vicar told me it was lived in during the war,' said Mr Annett. 'It housed a family of eight evacuees then. They didn't mind it being haunted, they told Mr Roberts.'

'Haunted?' we cried. I looked at Mr Annett to see if he was joking but his face was unusually thoughtful.

'It is, you know,' he said with conviction. 'I've seen the ghost myself. That's how I came to hear the history of the place from the vicar.'

'Is that why it stays empty?' I asked. It was strange that I had never heard this tale throughout my time at Fairacre.

Mr Annett laughed. 'No, indeed! I told you people lived in it for years. The evacuees said they'd sooner be haunted than bombed and spent all the war years here. I think Roberts found it just wasn't worth doing up after the war, and so it is now in this state.'

We looked again at the crumbling cottage. It was too small and homely to be sinister, despite this tale of a ghost. It had the pathetic look of a wild animal, tired to death, crouching in the familiar shelter of grass and neglected vegetation for whatever Fate might have in store.

'When did you see the ghost?' I asked.

Mr Annett sighed with mock importance. 'Persistent woman! I see I shall have no peace until I have put the whole uncomfortable proceedings before you. It was a very frightening experience indeed, and if you don't mind, I'll tell you the story as we walk. Even now my blood grows a little chilly at the memory. Brisk exercise is the right accompaniment for a ghost story.'

We continued up the lane, with young Malcolm now before and now behind us, scrambling up the banks and shouting with the sheer joy of living. With the scents of spring around us, and the soft wind lifting our hair, we listened to the tale of one strange winter night.

Every Friday night, with the exception of Good Friday, Mr Annett left the school house at Beech

Green and travelled the three miles to St Patrick's Church for choir practice.

Some men would have found it irksome to leave the comfort of their homes at seven in the evening and to face the windy darkness of a downland lane. Mr Annett was glad to do so. His love of music was strong enough to make his duty a positive pleasure, and although his impatient spirit chafed at times at the slow progress made by Fairacre's choir, he counted Friday evening as a highlight of the week.

At this time he had much need of comfort. He was a young widower, living alone in the school house, and ministered to by a middle-aged Scotswoman who came in daily. The death of his wife, six months after their marriage, was still too painful for him to dwell upon. She had been killed in an air raid, during the early part of the war, and for Mr Annett life would never be the same again.

One moonlit Friday evening in December, some years after the war had ended, he set out as usual for Fairacre. It was so bright that he could have driven his little car without headlights. The road glimmered palely before him, barred with black shadows where trees lined the road. He was early, for he had arranged to pick up some music from Miss Parr's house and knew that the old lady would want him to stop for a little time.

A maid opened the door. Miss Parr had been invited to her nephew's, but the music had been looked out for him, Mr Annett was told. He drove to St Patrick's, and went inside. It was cold and gloomy. No one had yet arrived, and Mr Annett decided to use his time in taking a stroll in the brilliant moonlight.

There was an unearthly beauty about the night that chimed with the young man's melancholy. He made his way slowly along a little-used lane near the church, and let sad memory carry him on its flood. It was not often that he so indulged himself. After his wife's death, he had moved to Beech Green and thrown himself, almost savagely, into school life. He had filled his time with work and music, so that he fell asleep with exhaustion rather than the numbing despair which had first governed every waking hour.

He passed a broken down cottage on his left, its remnants of thatch silvered with moonlight. Just beyond it a five-barred gate afforded a view of the distant downs. Mr Annett leant upon its topmost bar and surveyed the scene.

Before him lay the freshly ploughed fields, the furrows gleaming in the rays of the moon. Further away, a dusky copse made a black patch on the lower flanks of the downs. Against the clear sky

their mighty bulk looked more majestic than ever. There was something infinitely reassuring and comforting about their solidity, and the young man, gazing at them, let the tranquillity about him do its healing work.

It was very quiet. Far away, he heard a train hoot impatiently as it waited for a signal to allow its passage westward. Nearer, he was dimly conscious of the rustling of dead leaves at the foot of an old crab apple tree which stood hard by the gate. Some small nocturnal animal was foraging stealthily, wary of the silent man nearby.

Sunk in his thoughts, he was oblivious of the passage of time, and was hardly surprised to notice that a strange man had appeared in the lane without any noise of approach.

He came close to Mr Annett, nodded civilly, and leant beside him on the gate. For a moment, the two men rested silently side by side, elbows touching, and gazed at the silvered landscape before them. Despite the stranger's unexpected advent, Mr Annett felt little surprise. There was something gentle and companionable about the newcomer. The schoolmaster had the odd feeling that they were very much akin. Vaguely, he wondered if they had met before somewhere. He shifted along the gate – the stranger seemed excessively cold – and turned slightly to look at him.

He was a loosely-built fellow, of about Mr Annett's age, dressed in dark country clothes which seemed a pretty poor fit.

He wore an open-necked shirt and a spotted neckerchief, tied gipsy fashion, round his throat. He had a small beard, light in colour, which gleamed silver in the moonlight, and his fair hair was thick and wiry.

'Full moon tomorrow,' commented the stranger. For such a big man he had a remarkably small voice, Mr Annett noticed. It was almost falsetto, slightly husky and strained, as though he were suffering from laryngitis.

'So it is,' agreed Mr Annett.

They relapsed again into contemplation of the view. After some time, Mr Annett stirred himself long enough to find some cigarettes. He offered the packet to his companion.

'Thank'ee,' said the man. 'Thank'ee kindly, but I don't smoke these days.'

The schoolmaster lit his cigarette and surveyed the man. 'Haven't I seen you before somewhere?' he asked.

'Most likely. I've lived in Fairacre all my life,' answered the man huskily.

'I'm at Beech Green,' said Mr Annett.

The man drew in his breath sharply, as though in pain. 'My wife came from Beech Green,' he said. He bent his head forward suddenly. By the light of the moon Mr Annett saw that his eyes were closed. The use of the past tense was not lost upon the schoolmaster, himself still smarting with grief, and he led the conversation from the dangerous ground he had unwittingly encountered.

'Whereabouts in Fairacre do you live?' he asked.

The man raised his head and nodded briefly in the direction of the ruined cottage nearby. Mr Annett was puzzled by this, but thought that perhaps he was nodding generally in the direction of the village. Not wishing to distress him any further, and realizing that his choir must be soon arriving at St Patrick's, Mr Annett began to stir himself for departure. It was time he moved, in any case, for he had grown colder and colder since the arrival of the stranger, despite his warm overcoat. The stranger only had on a long jacket, but he seemed oblivious of the frost.

'Well, I must be off,' said Mr Annett. 'I'm due to take choir practice at seven thirty. Are you walking back to the village?'

The man straightened up and turned to face the schoolmaster. The moonlight shone full upon his face. It was a fine face, with high cheekbones and pale blue eyes set very wide apart. There was something Nordic in his aspect, with his great height and wide shoulders.

'I'll stop here a little longer,' he said slowly. 'This is the right place for me. I come most nights, particularly around full moon.'

'I can understand it,' said Mr Annett gently, scanning the sad grave face. 'There is comfort in a lovely place like this.'

A burst of laughter broke from the stranger's lips,

all the more uncanny for its cracked wheeziness. His wide-open eyes glittered in the moonlight.

'Comfort?' he echoed. 'There's no comfort for the likes of me – ever!' He began to tear savagely at the neckerchief about his throat. 'You can't expect comfort,' he gasped painfully, 'when you've done this to yourself!'

He pulled the cloth away with a jerk and tore his shirt opening away from the neck with both hands.

By the light of the moon, Mr Annett saw the livid scar which encircled his neck, the mark of a strangling rope which eternity itself could never remove.

He raised his horror-filled eyes to those of the stranger. They were still open, but they glittered no longer. They seemed to be dark gaping holes, full of mist, through which Mr Annett could dimly discern the outline of the crab apple tree behind him.

He tried to speak, but could not. And as he watched, still struggling for speech, the figure slowly dissolved, melting into thin air, until the schoolmaster found himself gazing at nothing at all but the old gnarled tree, and the still beauty of the night around it.

The vicar was alone in the vestry when Mr Annett arrived at St Patrick's.

'Good evening, good evening,' said the vicar bois-
terously, and then caught sight of his choirmaster's
face.

'My dear boy, you look as though you've seen a
ghost,' he said.

'You speak more truly than you realize,' Mr
Annett answered soberly. He began to walk through
to the chancel and his organ, but the vicar barred his
way. His kind old face was puckered with concern.

'Was it poor old Job?' he asked gently.

'I don't know who it was,' replied the schoolmaster. He explained briefly what had happened.
He was more shaken by this encounter than he
cared to admit. Somehow, the affinity between the
stranger and himself had seemed so strong. It made
the man's dreadful disclosure, and then his with-
drawal, even more shocking.

The vicar put both hands on the young man's
shoulders. 'Poor Job,' he said, 'is nothing to be
frightened of. It is a sad tale, and it happened long
ago. After choir practice, I hope you will come back
to the vicarage for a drink, and I will do my best to
tell you Job's story.'

The younger man managed a wan smile. 'Thank
you, Vicar,' he said. 'I should be glad to hear more
of him. I had a strange feeling while we were
together—' He faltered to a stop.

'What kind of feeling?' asked the vicar gently.

Mr Annett moved restlessly. His brow was furrowed with perplexity. 'As though – it sounds absurd – but as though we were brothers. It was as if we were akin – as if we shared something.'

The vicar nodded slowly, and sighed, dropping his hands from the young man's shoulders. 'You shared sorrow, my son,' he said as he turned away. But his tone was so low that the words were lost in a burst of country voices from the chancel.

Together the two men made their way from the vestry to the duties before them.

The vicarage drawing-room was empty when the vicar and his guest entered an hour or so later. A bright fire blazed on the hearth and Mr Annett gratefully pulled up an armchair. He felt as though he would never be warm again.

He sipped the whisky and water which the vicar gave him and was glad of its comfort. He was deathly tired, and recognized this as a symptom of shock. Part of his mind longed for sleep, but part craved to hear the story which the vicar had promised.

Before long, the older man put aside his glass,

lodged three stout logs upon the fire and settled back in his chair to recount his tale.

* * *

Job Carpenter, said the vicar, was a shepherd. He was born in Victoria's reign in the year of the Great Exhibition of 1851, and was the tenth child in a long family.

His parents lived in a small cottage at the Beech Green end of Fairacre, and all their children were born there. They were desperately poor, for Job's father was a farm labourer and times were hard.

At ten years old Job was out at work on the downs, stone-picking, bird-scaring and helping his father to clear ditches and lay hedges; but by the time he was fifteen he had decided that it was sheep he wanted to tend.

The shepherd at that time was a surly old fellow, twisted with rheumatism and foul of tongue. Job served a cruel apprenticeship under him and in the last year or two of the old man's life virtually looked after the flock himself. This fact did not go unnoticed by the farmer.

One morning during lambing time, Job entered the little hut carrying twin lambs which were weakly. There stretched upon the sacks stuffed with straw which made the old man's bed, lay his master, open-eyed and cold.

Within two days Job had been told that he was now shepherd, and he continued in this post for the rest of his life. He grew into a handsome fellow, tall and broad, with blond wiry hair and a curling beard. The girls of Fairacre and Beech Green found him attractive, and made the fact quite plain, but Job was shy and did not respond as readily as his fellows.

One day, however, he met a girl whom he had never seen before. Her family lived in Beech Green but she was in service in London. Job's sister worked with her and the two girls were given a week's

holiday at the same time. She walked over to see Job's sister one warm spring evening and the two girls wandered across the downs to see the lambs at play.

Job watched them approach. His sister Jane was tall and fair, as he was. Her companion was a complete contrast. She was little more than five feet in height, with long silky black hair coiled in a thick plait round her head, like a coronet. She had a small heart-shaped face, sloe-dark eyes which slanted upwards at the corners, and narrow crescents of eyebrows. Job thought her the prettiest thing he had ever seen.

Her name was Mary. To Job, who had a deep religious faith, this seemed wholly fitting. She was a queen among women. Job had no doubts this time and no shyness. Before Mary's week of holiday had ended the two young people came to an understanding.

It was Christmas time before they saw each other again, and only a few letters, written for them by better-schooled friends, passed between Mary and Job during the long months of separation. They planned to get married in the autumn of the following year. Mary would return to London and save every penny possible from her pitiful earnings, and Job would ask for a cottage of his own at Michaelmas.

He was fortunate. The farmer offered him a little thatched house not far from the church at Fairacre. It had two rooms up and two down, and a sizeable triangle of garden where a man could grow plenty of vegetables, keep a pig and a few hens, and so go more than half way towards being self-supporting. A few fruit trees shaded the garden, and a lusty young crab-apple tree grew in the hedge nearby.

The couple married at Michaelmas and were as happy as larks in their new home. Mary took work at the vicarage and found it less arduous than the living-in job in London. She was a quick quiet worker in the house and the vicar's wife approved of her. She was delighted to discover that her new daily was also an excellent needlewoman, and Mary found herself carrying home bundles of shirts whose collars needed turning, sheets that needed sides to middling, and damask table linen in need of fine darning. She was particularly glad of this extra money for by the end of the first year of their married life a child was due, and Mary knew she would have to give up the scrubbing and heavy lifting for a few weeks at least.

The coming of the child was of intense joy to Job. He adored his wife and made no secret of it. The fact that he cleaned her shoes and took her tea in bed in the mornings was known in Fairacre and looked upon as a crying scandal, particularly by the men. What was a woman for but to wait upon her menfolk? Job Carpenter was proper daft to pander to a wife in that namby-pamby way. Only laying up a store of trouble for himself in the future, said the village wiseacres in The Beetle and Wedge. Job, more in love than ever, let such gossip flow by him.

The baby took its time in coming and as soon as Job saw it he realized that it could not possibly survive. His experience with hundreds of lambs gave him a pretty shrewd idea of a 'good do-er' or a weakling. Mary, cradling it in her arms, smiling with happiness, suspected nothing. It was all the more tragic for her when, on the third day, her little son quietly expired.

She lay in a raging fever for a fortnight, and it was months before she was herself again. Throughout the time Job nursed her with loving constancy, comforting her when she wept, encouraging any spark of recovery.

In the two years that followed, two miscarriages occurred and the young couple began to wonder if they would ever have a family. The cottage gave them great joy, and the garden was one of the prettiest in the village, but it was a child that they really wanted. Everyone liked the Carpenters and Job's demonstrative affection for his wife was looked upon with more indulgence by the villagers as time passed.

At last Mary found that she was pregnant yet again. The vicar's wife, for whom she still worked, was determined that this baby should arrive safely, and insisted on Mary being examined regularly by her own doctor. She engaged too a reputable midwife from Caxley to attend the birth, for the local midwife at that time, in Fairacre and Beech Green, was a slatternly creature, reeking of gin and unwashed garments, whose very presence caused revulsion rather than reassurance to her unfortunate patients.

All went well. The baby was a lusty boy, who throve from the time he entered the world. Job and Mary could hardly believe their good fortune and peered into his cot a hundred times a day to admire his fair beauty.

One early October day, when the child was a few months old, Mary was sitting at the table with a pile of mending before her. The boy lay asleep in his cradle beside her.

It was a wild windy day. The autumn equinox had stirred the weather to tempestuous conditions, and the trees in the little garden flailed their branches in the uproar. Leaves whirled by the cottage window and every now and again a spatter of hail hit the glass like scattered shot. The doors rattled, the thin curtains stirred in the draught, and the whole cottage shuddered in the force of the gale. Mary was nervous, and wondered how poor Job was faring outside in the full force of the unkind elements.

As the afternoon wore on, the gale increased. Mary had never known such violence. There was a roaring noise in the chimney which was terrifying and a banshee howling of wind round the house which woke the baby and made him cry. Mary lifted him from his cradle to comfort him, and walked back and forth with him against her shoulder.

There was a sudden increase in the noise outside – a curious drumming sound in the heart of the fury. To Mary's horror she saw through the window the

small chicken house at the end of the garden swept upward and carried, twisting bizarrely, into the field beyond. At the same time a great mass of straw, clearly torn from a nearby rick, went whirling across the garden, and, as it passed, one of the apple trees, laden with golden fruit, snapped off at the base as though it were a flower stem.

Mary could scarcely believe her eyes. She stood rooted to the spot, between the table and the fireplace, her baby clutched to her. The drumming sound grew louder until it was unendurable. Mary was about to scream with panic when a terrifying rumble came near at hand. The chimney stack crashed upon the cottage roof, cracking the rafters like matchwood, and sending ceilings, furniture, bricks and rubble cascading upon the two terror-stricken occupants of the little home.

When Job arrived at the scene of the disaster, soaked to the skin and wild with anxiety, he found the whole of one end of his house had collapsed. No one was there, for the neighbours were all coping with troubles of their own, and there had been no time to see how others were faring in the catastrophe that had befallen Fairacre in the matter of minutes.

He began tearing at the beams and sagging thatch

with his bare hands, shouting hoarsely to his wife and son as he struggled. There was no answer to his cries. A ghastly silence seemed to pervade the ruined house, in contrast to the fiendish noises which raged about it.

An hour later, when neighbours arrived to help, they found him there, still screaming and struggling to reach his dead family. Sweat and tears poured down his ravaged face, his clothes were torn, his battered hands bleeding. When, finally, the broken bodies of his wife and child were recovered, Job had to be led away, and only the doctor's drugs brought him merciful oblivion at the end of that terrible day.

In the weeks that followed, while his house was being repaired, Job was offered hospitality throughout Fairacre but he would have none of it. As soon as the pitiful funeral was over, he returned numbly to his work, coming back each night to his broken home and sleeping on a makeshift bed in the one remaining room.

Neighbours did their best for him, cooking him a meal, washing his linen, comforting him with friendly words and advice. He seemed scarcely to see or to hear them, and heads shook over Job's sad plight.

'There's naught can help him, but time,' said one.

''Tis best to let him get over his grief alone,' said another.

'Once he gets his house set to rights, he'll start to pick up,' said a third. Fairacre watched poor Job anxiously.

The men who had been sent to repair the cottage worked well and quickly. Their sympathy was stirred by the sight of the gaunt young man's lonely existence in the undamaged half of his tiny house.

At length the living room was done. The bricks which had crashed on that fateful afternoon had been built again into the chimney breast. The broken rafters had been replaced, the walls plastered and whitewashed afresh.

Job met the men as he trudged home from work. They called to him with rough sympathy.

'It's ready for you now,' they shouted through the twilight.

'We've finished at last.'

A kindly neighbour had gone in to replace his furniture.

'There now,' she said, in a motherly burr, 'you can settle in here tonight.' But Job shook his head, and turned into his old room.

Sad at heart, the good soul returned home, but could not forget the sight of Job's ravaged face.

'I'll go and take a look at him,' she said to her husband later that evening. 'If the lamp's alight in the room then I'll know he's settled in, and I'll go more comfortable to bed.'

But the window was dark. She was about to turn homeward again when she heard movements inside the cottage and saw the living-room door open. Job stood upon the threshold, a candle in his hand. Breathless, in the darkness of the garden, the watcher saw him make his way slowly across the room to the chimney breast. He put down the guttering candle, and rested his fair head against the brick-work. Before long, his great shoulders began to heave, and the sound of dreadful sobbing sent the onlooker stealthily homeward.

''Tis best by far to leave him be,' comforted the neighbour's husband, when she told him what she had witnessed. 'We'll go and see him in the morning. It will be all over by then.'

But there was little comfort for the woman that night, for the spectacle of Job's grief drove all hope of sleep away.

Next morning they went together to the house. Her heart was heavy with foreboding as they walked up the little brick path. Inside the silent house they found him, with a noose about his neck, hanging against the chimney breast which had crushed his wife, his child, and every hope of Job himself.

* * *

There was an uncanny silence in the sunny lane as Mr Annett finished speaking.

'And that,' he said soberly, 'is the tale of poor Job, as the vicar told it to me.'

Suddenly, a blackbird called from a hazel bush, breaking the spell. Despite the sunshine I shivered. We were alone, for Malcolm and his mother had gone ahead to pick primroses from the steep banks, and though we were surrounded by the sights and scents of spring I remained chilled by this strange winter's tale.

'You're sure it was a ghost?' I asked shakily.

'Other people have seen Job,' answered Mr Annett, 'and the vicar knew all about him. But I believe I am the only person that Job has spoken to.'

'I wonder why?' I mused aloud.

'Perhaps he felt we had much in common,' said Mr Annett quietly.

I remembered suddenly Mr Annett's own tragedy. He, too, had adored a young wife and had lost her in the face of overwhelming violence. He too had watched a broken body removed to an early grave. There was no misery, no depth of hopelessness which Job had known, which was not known too to young Mr Annett.

We were summoned abruptly from the shadowy past by the sound of young Malcolm's excited voice.

'There's a nest here,' he called, 'with eggs. Come and look!'

'Coming!' shouted Mr Annett, suddenly looking ten years younger. And he ran off, all grief forgotten, to join his wife and child.

Christmas at Caxley
1913

Illustrated by J. S. Goodall

*T*he market square of Caxley is the hub of that country town. It is here that its inhabitants meet in times of national rejoicing or disaster. On market day the local buses rumble in from the surrounding villages, from Fairacre and Beech Green in the north, and from Bent and its neighbours in the south. The people come to meet their friends, to do business, to seek bargains, and 'to see a bit of life'.

At the turn of the century, two families lived in Caxley market square in the premises above and behind their shops. One was the Howards, and Septimus Howard, the local baker, was its head. The other was the Norths, long-established ironmongers, and Bender North carried on a flourishing business.

The two men had been born and bred in Caxley, had attended the same school, played football together and married local girls. Hilda North was a pillar of the parish church, and much respected. Edna Howard was a flamboyant beauty, and local opinion held that Septimus was a most unlikely candidate for her favours when he was pursuing her. But he had won her eventually, and the marriage had prospered.

The children of the two families grew up together, and helped when they could in the family businesses.

As King Edward VII's reign continued, Septimus's modest business grew apace. Bender's began to decline, for a large national firm of ironmongers opened a branch in Caxley High Street, and many of his old clients, particularly farmers, began to take their custom to Tenby's Ltd who were bringing a wide variety of new agricultural machinery to local notice.

By the winter of 1913 Bender North was a worried man, and another blow came when Bob, a trusted employee, absconded with a great deal of money.

In the meantime, Septimus Howard was cautiously assessing his good fortune, and continuing to work as zealously as ever.

*

There was plenty of work at the bakery as Christmas approached, for there were scores of large cakes to be iced, as well as extra supplies for family parties.

Although Septimus now employed several more workers, he still did as much himself in the bakery. The fragrance of the rich mixtures, the mingled aroma of spices, candied fruits and brown sugar cheered him afresh every year. It was his own personal offering to the spirit of Christmas, and he enjoyed the festive bustle in the warmly-scented bakery. It was a sheltered haven from the bleak winds which whistled across the market square beyond the doors.

The cold spell was lasting longer than expected, and the weather-wise old folk in Caxley prophesied a white Christmas. Sure enough, in the week before Christmas, a light fall whitened the ground, and powdered the rosy-tiled roofs of the town, while the lowering grey skies told of more to follow.

On Sunday afternoon, Sep took a nap on his bed. Edna had slipped out to visit friends and, unusually tired by the pre-Christmas work, Sep indulged himself.

When he awoke, he was conscious of a new lightness in the room. He made his way to the bedroom window. His hair was rumpled from his rare

afternoon nap. He smoothed it as he watched the snow flakes fluttering against the window pane.

He judged that it was two or three inches deep already. The steps of St Peter's and the Town Hall were heavily carpeted. The snow had blown into the cracks and jambs of doors and windows, leaving long white sticks like newly-spilt milk. A mantle of snow draped Queen Victoria's shoulders and her bronze crown supported a little white cushion which looked like ermine. Snow lay along her sceptre and in the folds of her robes. The iron cups, in the fountain at her feet, were filled to the brim with snow flakes, and the embossed lions near by peered from snow-encrusted manes.

For a Sunday afternoon, there were very few people about. An old tramp, carrying his belongings in a red-spotted bundle on a stick, snuffled disconsolately past St Peter's, head bent, rheumy eyes fixed upon the snow at his feet. Two ragged urchins, no doubt from the marsh, giggled and barged each other behind him, scraping up the snow in red, wet hands to make snowballs.

Sep watched them heave them at the back of the unsuspecting old man. At the moment of impact, he swung round sharply, and raised his bundle threateningly. Sep could see his red, wet, toothless mouth protesting, but could hear no word through the tightly-shut bedroom window. One boy put his thumb to his nose impudently; the other put out his tongue. But they let the old man shuffle round the corner unmolested before throwing their arms round each other's skinny shoulders and running jubilantly down an alley-way.

Momentarily the market square was empty. Not even a pigeon pattered across the snow. Only footprints of various sizes, and the yellow stain made by a horse's urine, gave any sign of life in that white world. Snow clothed the sloping roofs of Caxley. It covered the hanging signs and the painted name-boards above the shops, dousing the bright colours as a candle-snuffer douses a light.

What a grey and white world, thought Sep! As grey and white as an old gander, as grey and white as the swans and cygnets floating together on the Cax. The railings outside the bank stood starkly etched against the white background, each spear-top tipped with snow. There was something very soothing in this negation of colour and movement. It reminded Sep of creeping beneath the bedclothes as a child, and crouching there, in a soft, white haven, unseeing and unseen, all sounds muffled, as he relished the secrecy and security of it all.

There was a movement in St Peter's porch and a dozen or so choirboys came tumbling out into the snowy world, released from carol practice. The sight brought Sep, sighing, back into the world of Sunday afternoon.

He picked up a hair-brush and began to attack his tousled locks.

'Looks as though the weather prophets are right,' said Sep to his reflection. 'Caxley's in for a white Christmas this year.'

*

On that same Sunday afternoon Bender North set off to deliver two large saw blades for his old farmer friend Jesse Miller of Fairacre and Beech Green.

'He won't get much done in the fields,' commented Bender, wrapping the blades in brown paper. 'The ground's like iron. He'll be glad to set the men to sawing firewood tomorrow, and I promised him these as soon as they came.'

'Wrap up warmly,' said Hilda. 'Put your muffler on, and your thick gloves.'

'Never fear,' answered Bender robustly. 'I've known the downs long enough to know how to dress for them. I'll be back before dark.'

The horse trotted briskly through the town. There were very few people about and Bender was glad to be on his own in the clean fresh air. Now he could turn over his thoughts, undisturbed by family interruptions or customers' problems. He always felt at his best driving behind a good horse. He liked the rhythm of its flying feet, the gay rattle of the bowling wheels, and the clink of the well-polished harness.

The pace slackened as Bill, the horse, approached Beech Green. The long pull up the downs was taken gently and steadily. The reins lay loosely across the glossy back, and Bender reviewed his situation as they jogged along together through the grey and white countryside.

Things were serious, that was plain. Bob, the thief, had been picked up by the London police ten days earlier, and now awaited his trial at the next Assizes. He had been in possession of fourteen shillings and ninepence at the time of his arrest, and could not – or would not – give any idea of where the rest of the money had gone. Clearly, nothing would be restored to his employer.

What would he do, Bender asked himself? He could get a further loan from the bank, but would it be of any use? Had the time come to take a partner who would be willing to put money into the firm? Bender disliked the idea. He could approach both Sep Howard and Jesse Miller who had offered help, but he hated the thought of letting Sep Howard see his straits, and he doubted whether Jesse Miller could afford to give him the sum needed to give the business a fresh start. Jesse was in partnership with his brother Harry at the farm, and times were hard for them both at the moment.

The other course was a much more drastic one. Tenby's had approached him with a tentative offer. If he ever decided to part with the business, would he give them first offer? He would of course be offered a post with the firm who would be glad of his experience. They were thinking of housing their agricultural machinery department in separate premises. North's, in the market square, handy for all the farmers in the district, would suit them perfectly. They asked Bender to bear it in mind. Bender had thought of little else for two days, but had said nothing to Hilda. He knew that she would be all in favour of the action, and he wanted to be sure that it was right before making any final decisions.

He presumed that he would be offered the managership. In that case, there would be a steady income, with no worries attached. Bender, gazing unseeingly across the snowy fields, lulled almost into slumber by the rhythmic swaying of the trap, began to feel that selling North's might be the best way out of his many difficulties. But not yet, he told himself. He would hang on as long as he could, and who knows? Something might turn up. He'd been lucky often enough before. There was still hope! Bender North was always an optimist.

He put Billy into the shelter of a stable and tramped across the snowy yard to the Millers' back door.

He was greeted warmly by the family, and he was put by the fire to thaw out. The usual vast tea was offered him, but Bender ate sparingly, with one eye cocked on the grey threatening sky outside.

'I mustn't be too long,' said Bender, his mouth full of buttered toast. 'There's more snow to come before morning, or I'll eat my boots.'

They exchanged family news. Ethel's youngest was running a temperature, and was upstairs in bed, 'very fretful and scratchity', his mother said. Jesse's pigs were not doing as well as he had hoped, and he had an idea that one of his men was taking eggs. 'Times were bad enough for farmers,' said Jesse, 'without such set-backs.'

He accompanied Bender to the stable when he set off.

'And how are your affairs?' he asked when they were out of earshot of the house.

Bender gave a reassuring laugh, and clapped the other man's shoulders. 'Better than they have been, Jesse, I'm glad to say. I hope I shan't have to worry you at all.'

The look of relief that flooded Jesse's face did not escape Bender. It certainly looked as though Tenby's would be the only possible avenue of escape if the business grew worse.

Ah well, thought Bender, clattering across the cobbled yard, we must just live in hope of something turning up! He waved to Jesse, and set off at a spanking pace on the downhill drive home.

The snow began to fall as Bender turned out of

Jesse's gate. It came down thickly and softly, large flakes flurrying across mile upon mile of open downland, like an undulating lacy curtain. It settled rapidly upon the iron-hard ground, already sheeted in the earlier fall, and by the time Billy had covered half a mile the sound of his trotting hoofs was muffled. He snorted fiercely at the onslaught of this strange element, his breath bursting from his flaring nostrils in clouds of vapour. His dark mane was starred with snow flakes, and as he tossed his head Bender caught a glimpse of his shining eyes grotesquely ringed with glistening snow caught in his eyelashes.

His own face was equally assaulted. The snow flakes fluttered against his lips and eyes like icy moths. It was difficult to breathe. He pulled down the brim of his hard hat, and hoisted up the muffler that Hilda had insisted on him wearing, so that he could breathe in the stuffy pocket of air made by his own warmth. Already the front of his coat was plastered, and he looked like a snowman.

A flock of sheep, in a field, huddled together looking like one vast fleece ribbed with snow. The bare hedges were fast becoming blanketed, and the banks undulated past the bowling trap smoothly white, but for the occasional pock-mark of a bird's claws. The tall dry grasses bore strange exotic white flowers in their dead heads, and the branches of trees collected snowy burdens in their arms.

And all the time there was a rustling and whispering, a sibilance of snow. The air was alive with movement, the dancing and whirling of a thousand individual flakes with a life as brief as the distance from leaden sky to frozen earth. At the end of their tempestuous short existence they lay together, dead and indivisible, forming a common shroud.

There was a grandeur and beauty about this snowy countryside which affected Bender deeply. Barns and houses, woods and fields were now only massive white shapes, their angles smoothed into gentle curves. He passed a cow-man returning from milking, his head and shoulders shrouded in a sack, shaped like a monk's cowl. He was white from head to foot, only his dark eyes, glancing momentarily at the passing horse, and his plodding gait distinguished him from the white shapes about him.

Bender turned to watch him vanishing into the veil of swirling flakes. Behind him, the wheels were spinning out two grey ribbons, along the snowy road.

He turned back and flicked the reins on Billy's snow-spattered satin back.

'Gee up boy!' roared Bender cheerfully. 'We both want to get home!'

Jingle Bells

Illustrated by J. S. Goodall

Mr Willet, the school caretaker, was brushing up coke in the yard as I went across to the school that morning. He was wielding the broom vigorously in his capable hands, his breath wreathing his head in silvery clouds.

'Nasty cold morning,' I called to him, scurrying towards shelter.

'This keeps me warm,' he replied, pausing for a moment to rest on his broom. 'But I s'pose I shan't be doing this much longer.'

'Only three days,' I agreed. 'And then it's the lovely Christmas holidays!'

'You should be ashamed!' said Mr Willet

reproachfully. 'Young woman like you, wishing your life away.'

But it was too cold to argue, and I only had time to wave to him before whisking into the shelter of the lobby.

The last day of term, particularly the Christmas term, has splendour of its own. There is an air of excitement at the thought of pleasures and freedom to come, but there is also a feeling of relaxation from daily routine made much more acute by the deliciously empty desks. Books have been collected and stacked in neat piles in the cupboard. Papers and exercise books have been tidied away. All that remains to employ young hands in this last glorious day is a pencil and loose sheets of paper which have been saved for just such an occasion.

Of course, work will be done. There will be mental arithmetic, and some writing; perhaps some spelling lists and paper games, and stories told to each other. And today, the children knew, there would be Christmas carols, and a visit to the old grey church next door to see the crib recently set up by the vicar's wife and other ladies of the village. The very thought of it all created a glow which warmed the children despite the winter's cold.

They entered more exuberantly than ever, cherry-nosed, hair curling damply from the December air and wellingtons plastered with Fairacre mud. I began to shoo them back into the lobby before our virago of a cleaner discovered them, but I was too late.

Mrs Pringle, emerging from the infants' room where she had just deposited a scuttle of coke on an outspread sheet of *The Times Educational Supplement*, looked at them with marked dislike.

'Anyone 'ere seen fit to use the door-scraper?' she asked sourly. 'Don't look like it to me. What you kids wants is an hour or two scrubbing this 'ere floor like I 'ave to. That'd make you think twice about dirtying my clean floorboards.'

She cast a malevolent glance in my direction and stumped out to the lobby. The children retreated before her, observing her marked limp, a sure sign of trouble.

The clatter of the door-scraper and the bang of the heavy Gothic door announced Mrs Pringle's departure to her cottage, until midday, when she was due to return to wash up the school dinner things. The children's spirits rose again and they sang 'Away in a Manger' with rather more gusto than perhaps was necessary at prayer time.

The infants departed to their own side of the

partition and my class prepared to give part of its mind to some light scholastic task. Multiplication tables are always in sore need of attention, as every teacher knows, so that a test on the scrap paper already provided seemed a useful way of passing the arithmetic lesson. It was small wonder that excitement throbbed throughout the classroom. The paper chains still rustled overhead in all their multi-coloured glory and in the corner, on the now depleted nature table, the Christmas tree glittered with tinsel and bright baubles.

But this year it carried no parcels. Usually, Fairacre School has a party on the last afternoon of the Christmas term when mothers and fathers, and friends of the school, come and eat a hearty tea and watch the children receive their presents from the tree. But this year the party was to be held in the village hall after Christmas and a conjuror had been engaged to entertain us afterwards.

However, the children guessed that they would not go home empty-handed today, I felt sure, and this touching faith, which I had no intention of destroying, gave them added happiness throughout the morning.

The weather grew steadily worse. Sleet swept across the playground and a wicked draught from the skylight buffeted the paper chains. I put the milk saucepan on the tortoise stove and the children looked pleased. Although a few hardy youngsters gulp their milk down stone-cold, even on the iciest day, most of them prefer to be cosseted a little and to see their bottles being tipped into the battered saucepan. The slow heating of the milk affords them exquisite pleasure, and it usually gets more attention than I do on cold days.

'It's steaming, miss,' one calls anxiously.

'Shall I make sure the milk's all right?' queries another.

'Can I get the cups ready?' asks a third.

One never-to-be-forgotten day we left the milk on whilst we had a rousing session in the playground as aeroplanes, galloping horses, trains and other violently moving articles. On our return, breathless and much invigorated, we had discovered a sizzling seething mess on the top of the stove and sticky cascades down the sides. Mrs Pringle did not let any of us forget this mishap, and the children like to pretend that they only keep reminding me to save me from incurring the lady's wrath yet again.

In between sips of their steaming milk they kept up an excited chatter.

'What d'you want for Christmas?' asked Patrick of Ernest, his desk mate.

'Boxing gloves,' replied Ernest, lifting his head briefly and speaking through a white moustache.

'Well, I'm havin' a football, and a space helmet, and some new crayons, and a signal box for my train set,' announced Patrick proudly.

Linda Moffat, neat as a new pin from glossy hair to equally glossy patent leather slippers, informed me that she was hoping for a new work-box with a pink lining. I thought of the small embroidery scissors, shaped like a stork, which I had wrapped up for her the night before, and congratulated myself.

'What do you want?' I asked Joseph Coggs, staring monkey-like at me over the rim of his mug.

'Football,' croaked Joseph, in his hoarse gipsy voice. 'Might get it too.'

It occurred to me that this would make an excellent exercise in writing and spelling. Milk finished, I set them to work on long strips of paper.

'Ernest wants some boxing gloves for Christmas,' was the first entry.

'Patrick hopes to get—' began the second. The children joined in the list-making with great enthusiasm.

When Mrs Crossley, who brings the dinners, arrived, she was cross-questioned about her hopes.

'Well now, I don't really know,' she confessed, balancing the tins against her wet mackintosh and peering perplexedly over the top. 'A kitchen set, I think. You know, a potato masher and fish slice and all that, in a nice little rack.'

The children obviously thought this a pretty poor present but began to write down: 'Mrs Crossley wants a kitchen set,' below the last entry, looking faintly disbelieving as they did so.

'And what do you want?' asked Linda, when Mrs Crossley had vanished.

'Let me see,' I said slowly: 'Some extra nice soap, perhaps, and bath cubes; and a book or two, and a new rose bush to plant by my back door.'

'Is that all?'

'No sweets?'

'No, no sweets,' I said. 'But I should like a very pretty little ring I saw in Caxley last Saturday.'

'You'll have to get married for that,' said Ernest soberly. 'And you're too old now.' The others nodded in agreement.

'You're probably right,' I told them, keeping a straight face. 'Put your papers away and let's set the tables for dinner.'

The sleet was cruelly painful on our faces as we scuttled across the churchyard to St Patrick's. Inside it was cold and shadowy. The marble memorial tablets on the wall glimmered faintly in the gloom, and the air struck chill.

But the crib was aglow with rosy light, a spot of warmth and hope in the darkness. The children tiptoed towards it, awed by their surroundings.

They spent a long time gazing, whispering their admiration and pointing out particular details to each other. They were loth to leave it, and the shelter of the great church, which had defied worse weather than this for many centuries.

We pelted back to the school, for I had a secret plan to put into action, and three o'clock was the time appointed for it. St Patrick's clock chimed a quarter to, above our heads, as we hurried across the churchyard.

I had arranged with the infants' teacher to go privately into the lobby promptly at three and there shake some bells abstracted earlier from the percussion band box. We hoped that the infants would believe that an invisible Father Christmas had driven on his sleigh and delivered the two sacks of parcels which would be found in the lobby. At the moment, these were in the hall of my house. I proposed to leave my class for a minute, shake the bells, hide them from inquisitive eyes and return again to the children.

This innocent deception could not hope to take in many of my own children, I felt sure, but the babies would enjoy it, and so too would the younger ones in my classroom. I was always surprised at the remarkable reticence which the older children showed when the subject of Father Christmas cropped up. Those that knew seemed more than willing to keep up the pretence for the sake of the younger ones, and perhaps because they feared that the presents would not be forthcoming if they let the cat out of the bag or boasted of their knowledge.

I settled the class with more paper. They could draw a picture of the crib or St Patrick's church, or a winter scene of any kind, I told them. Someone wanted to go on with his list of presents and was readily given permission. The main thing was to have a very quiet classroom at three o'clock. Our Gothic doors are of sturdy oak and the sleigh bells would have to be shaken to a frenzy in order to make themselves heard.

At two minutes to three by the wall clock Patrick looked up from drawing a church with all four sides showing at once, and surmounted by what looked like a mammoth ostrich.

'I've got muck on my hand,' he said. 'Can I go out the lobby and wash?'

Maddening child! What a moment to choose! 'Not now,' I said, as calmly as I could. 'Just wipe it on your hanky.'

He produced a dark grey rag from his pocket and rubbed the offending hand, sighing in a martyred way. He was one of the younger children and I wondered if he might possibly half-believe in sleigh bells.

'I'm just going across to the house,' I told them, squaring my conscience. 'Be very quiet while I'm away. The infants are listening to a story.'

All went according to plan. I struggled back through the sleet with the two sacks, deposited one outside the infants' door into the lobby, and the other outside our own.

The lobby was as quiet as the grave. I withdrew the bells from behind a stack of bars of yellow soap which Mrs Pringle stores on a lofty shelf, and crept to the outside door to begin shaking. Santa Claus in the distance, and fast approaching, I told myself. Would they be heard? I wondered, waggling frantically in the open doorway.

I closed the door gently against the driving sleet and now shook with all my might by the two inner doors. Heaven help me if one of my children burst out to see what was happening!

There was an uncanny silence from inside both rooms. I gave a last magnificent agitation and then crept along the lobby to the soap and tucked the bells securely out of sight. Then I returned briskly to the classroom. You could have heard a pin drop.

'There was bells outside,' said Joseph huskily.

'The clock just struck three,' I pointed out, busying myself at the blackboard.

'No. *Little* bells!' said someone.

At this point the dividing door between the infants' room and ours burst open to reveal a bright-eyed mob lugging a sack.

'Father Christmas has been!'

'We heard him!'

'We heard bells, didn't we?'

'That's right. Sleigh bells.'

Ernest, by this time, had opened our door into the lobby and was returning with the sack. A cheer went up and the whole class converged upon him.

'Into your desks,' I bellowed, 'and Ernest can give them out.'

Ernest upended the sack and spilt the contents into a glorious heap of pink and blue parcels, as the children scampered to their desks and hung over them squeaking with excitement.

The babies sat on the floor receiving their presents with awed delight. There was no doubt about it, for them Father Christmas was as real as ever.

I became conscious of Patrick's gaze upon me.

'Did you see him?' he asked.

'Not a sign,' I said truthfully.

Patrick's brow was furrowed with perplexity. 'If you'd a let me wash my hand I reckon I'd just about've seen him,' he said at length.

I made no reply. Patrick's gaze remained fixed on my face, and then a slow lovely smile curved his countenance. Together, amidst the hubbub of parcel-opening around us, we shared the unspoken, immortal secret of Christmas.

Later, with the presents unwrapped and the floor a sea of paper, Mrs Pringle arrived to start clearing up. Her face expressed considerable disapproval and her limp was very severe.

The children thronged around her showing her their toys.

'Ain't mine lovely?'

'Look, it's a dust cart!'

'This is a *magic* painting book! It says so!'

Mrs Pringle unbent a little among so much happiness, and gave a cramped smile.

Ernest raised his voice as she limped her way slowly across the room. 'Mrs Pringle, Mrs Pringle!'

The lady turned, a massive figure ankle deep in pink and blue wrappings.

'What do you want in your stocking, Mrs Pringle?' called Ernest. There was a sudden hush.

Mrs Pringle became herself again. 'In my stocking?' she asked tartly. 'A new leg! That's what I want!'

She moved majestically into the lobby, pretending to ignore the laughter of the children at this sally.

As usual, I thought wryly, Mrs Pringle had had the last word.

The White Robin

Illustrated by J. S. Goodall

To Macdonald Hastings
who gave me the idea

CHAPTER ONE

The Visitation

Village schools get rarer every year, but there are a small number, up and down the country, which still look much the same as they did some hundred years ago.

Fairacre School, where I am the headmistress, is one of them. It has, in common with many other country schools, the inestimable joy of a playground where the surrounding countryside invades the small patch of asphalt.

How lucky we are! The town child goes out to play at break-time on a vast, arid waste, criss-crossed with painted lines for various games, and rarely boasting even one desiccated plane tree. He would be hard put to it to find even a modest wood louse in this desert, whilst we in Fairacre enjoy the company of the birds and insects which share the trees, the meadows and the cornfields around us.

We are blessed with a fine clump of lofty trees which gives us shade at one side of the playground, a hedge of hawthorn and hazel which provides cover for the birds, and a dark corner where the play-ground touches the adjoining garden wall of the vicarage.

This secret haunt is the favourite place to play. Here grow, in wild confusion, all those rank plants and shrubs which flourish on neglect.

Elder trees, their bark criss-crossed and green, wave their ghostly flower heads in the shade, and fill the air with spicy scent.

On the vicar's side of the flint wall, mounds of rotting grass cuttings have accumulated over the years, providing a perfect habitat for outsize stinging nettles and majestic dock plants which raise their rusty spires above the wall. Little ferns grow from the crevices and, along the top, strips of moss like velvet ribbon flourish between the ancient coping bricks. Here and there great swags of ivy hang down on each side, the twisted ropey stems provid-ing footholds for the inquisitive ones wanting to peer over the wall.

On our side of the wall, the same plants thrive, but we also have some blue periwinkles and some par-ticularly hardy yellow aconites which some long-dead gardener must have introduced, and which seem to enjoy their murky surroundings.

Above all, spreading its arms in general blessing upon ecclesiastical and scholastic territory, is a superb oak tree, drawing nourishment, no doubt, from the vicar's grass cuttings and from the neighbouring churchyard with its mossy headstones.

Invariably, there are a few children enjoying this shady retreat. It is a fine place to rest after a spirited assault on the coke pile at the other side of the playground. There are always plenty of snails there, some small and elegant with pale yellow and brown shells, and many more of the common or garden variety, laboriously clambering up the wall and leaving their silver trails across the flints.

And in their wake come the birds. Blackbirds and thrushes, wrens and robins, raucous starlings and ubiquitous sparrows all haunt the bushes for food, and also for places to nest in this delectable spot. It is no wonder that the children find it so attractive. Around them stretch open cornfields and meadows. The great bulk of the downs lies on their horizon some two or three miles distant. Under a vast sky, the open countryside shimmers in a heat haze in summer and endures the onslaught of bitter winds in winter. This enclosed and secret place, mysteriously quiet, the haven of shy wild things, is in complete contrast to the bracing downland in which they live, and is prized accordingly.

And it was here that one of the Coggs twins first saw what I brusquely dismissed as 'her vision'.

*

It was a day of July heat, with the end of the school year in sight. The schoolroom door was propped open with a piece of sarsen stone as big as child's head. We had already used the object as the theme for a useful lesson on the derivation of words, although I had the feeling that my explanation of 'Saracen', meaning a foreigner, turning into 'sarsen' had been only partially accepted. In this heat the children were more than usually lethargic, their minds running, no doubt, on the joys of the open air rather than the schoolroom.

From outside came the sounds of high summer. A posse of young blackbirds kept up a piping for food, following their hard-working parents, tattered now with weeks of child care, hither and thither across the playground. In the distance the metallic croak of a pheasant could be heard, and over all was the faint hum of a myriad flying insects.

The languorous hush was broken by Helen Coggs who raised a hand. It was the usual request, and I was swift to grant it. The Coggs children seem to need to visit the lavatory twice as frequently as the others, but they are poorly fed and poorly clothed, the product of two feckless and unhealthy parents, so that their little weakness is not surprising.

'You can take out your library books,' I told the class, as Helen vanished across the playground. It was pointless to try and compete with the heat. My efforts to enliven the derivation of 'sarsen' had met with so little response that I felt that their library books might offer more palatable food on a hot July afternoon.

While they turned the pages languidly, I busied myself with some marking at my desk. I had forgotten about Helen, and it must have been some ten minutes later when she appeared at my side looking unusually lively.

'Oi bin and sin a whoite bird,' she declared. The fact that she had seen a white bird did not excite me greatly. It was probably a seagull, I thought. They come inland when conditions are rough by the coast. Or maybe one of Mr Roberts's white Leghorn hens, or a goose, had strayed.

'You've been long enough,' I scolded. 'Go and get on with your reading.'

Somewhat dashed, the child returned to her desk and took out her book. Peace reigned again, and I continued to mark.

But some minutes later I put down my red pencil. There was something odd about this white bird. Gulls would not be inland in this weather and, now I came to think of it, Mr Roberts, our local farmer,

had given up keeping chickens over a month ago. He still had a few geese, I believed. Could one have strayed so far?

'This bird,' I said to Helen. The class looked up. 'How big was it?'

'It was a little 'un.'

'It wasn't one of Mr Roberts's geese?'

'No.'

'You're sure it was white?'

'Yes.'

'Well, come on! Tell me how big it was.'

The child put her hands three inches apart, but said nothing.

Like getting blood out of a stone, I thought despairingly. Most of the Fairacre children are barely articulate. The Coggs children are monosyllabic at best.

The rest of the class now began to take an interest in the proceedings.

'Could it have been a white blackbird?' I enquired. Some years earlier we had been visited by a partially albino blackbird. At this my class began to guffaw.

'A *white* blackbird!' repeated Patrick, pink with mirth. 'How can a *black* bird be a *white* bird?'

'You sometimes get a blackbird with a few white feathers,' I explained, but the children were far too busy enjoying the joke to take much interest.

The clock told us it was playtime, and I decided to shelve the problem. In any case, no fowl of Mr Roberts seemed to be involved, which was my first concern. Also I had a suspicion that the white bird might have been some other object, a piece of paper fluttered by the wind, or a white flower head. With some of the children I might have suspected that the bird was a figment of a lively imagination, but not with Helen Coggs. She was quite incapable of such a flight of fancy.

The children streamed out into the sunshine, their spirits brightened by the prospect of fresh air and exercise, and the enjoyment of Helen Coggs's disclosure.

'Some ol' magpie, I bet,' said Ernest derisively, as he passed her on his way out. She shook her head.

The classroom soon emptied, except for Helen.

'Run along,' I said.

'It were a *little* bird. On the vicar's wall. Up the back.'

This was one of the longest speeches I had ever known the child deliver. 'Up the back' was the term used affectionately to describe the bosky haunt I have described. The lavatories are nearby, and the child must have spent some time after visiting them in exploring this much favoured area. But a white bird? Much more likely to be a head of elder flowers, now in full bloom, caught by an eddy of air and visible briefly over the wall. I must get the school doctor to test the child's eyes on her next visit.

'Don't worry about it,' I said. 'Go and enjoy the sunshine. If there is a white bird about, you will probably see it again some time.'

What a hope, I thought privately, as Helen moved off. It was highly unlikely that the apparition would be seen again.

But it was.

This time the vicar saw the white bird, and hastened into the school to report the sighting. The Reverend Gerald Partridge visits our school regularly, not only because he is chairman of the managers, but because he is our parish priest and the friend of all Fairacre.

Having told me the news in some excitement, he turned to the class.

'I've just been telling Miss Read that there is a rare white bird about. No doubt some of you have seen it?'

The children looked at each other in silence. Then Ernest nudged Helen's shoulder.

'I sin 'un,' muttered the child.

'Where, my dear?'

'Up the back.'

The vicar turned to me for clarification.

'By your wall,' I explained. 'Where the elder trees grow.'

'Ah! And all the weeds! Yes, I suspected as much. The robins must have nested there again this spring.'

'Do they nest there every year?'

'I can't say with any certainty, but the vicarage garden always seems to have one or two pairs each year, and very little fighting over territory. I imagine there is enough room for all. One pair built in the ivy on the wall some years ago. We found the nest later.'

'And are they there again?'

'Somewhere there, I feel sure. There are so many ideal sites in that wilderness, and we have certainly seen three or four fledglings being fed recently.'

He turned again to the class.

'Now, this little white bird seems rather shy, and it may well be attacked by other birds as it looks so different. I want you to be very careful not to frighten it in any way, and to let Miss Read, or me, know if you catch sight of it again.'

'Is it a foreign bird then?' hazarded Patrick.

'No, my boy. I rather think it is a robin – an *albino* robin. Albino means that it has no colour.'

Here he paused.

'At least, albino birds are usually all white, but in the case of the robin or the bullfinch the *red* feathers still keep their colour, so you can see how very beautiful a white robin must look.'

There was a stir of excitement among the children. A white robin, with a red breast! Here indeed was something rich and strange!

'I intend to find out more from Mr Mawne,' he told my class. Henry Mawne is an ornithologist of some standing, and lives in Fairacre. He is a good friend of the vicar's, and the church accounts have benefited from his meticulous attention. Before his coming they were in sad disarray, as our lovable vicar has no head for figures, and since the advent of decimalisation has been more bewildered than ever. Henry Mawne has relieved him of his financial duties, and the village is grateful to him.

'Perhaps he will come and give you a talk about birds – particularly robins. I will ask him. I know he has some splendid slides of British birds.'

He said goodbye to the children, and I accompanied him into the lobby.

'And you think this really is an albino robin?' I asked.

'I'm almost sure. I've caught a glimpse of it twice now, and the second time I had my binoculars. Its breast is quite a pale golden colour at the moment as the bird is so young, but it was being fed by a true robin, I'm positive. Isn't it exciting?'

His face was radiant.

'Think how beautiful it will look by next Christmas! We must take great care of it. I'm sure you will impress upon the children how fortunate we are to have such a wonderful bird among us.'

I promised, and was about to return to my class when the vicar stopped me.

'But you knew already, I suppose, about this bird? I mean the child Coggs said she had seen it.'

'I'm afraid I didn't believe her,' I confessed.

'Didn't believe her?' echoed the vicar, looking shocked. 'But she is a truthful child, surely?'

'She's truthful enough,' I agreed. 'But it seemed such an odd thing to see,' I added lamely. 'And no one else had seen it.'

'And so you doubted the child's word?' He looked sorrowfully at me. If he had caught me robbing the church poor box I could not have felt more guilty.

'There are some things,' he continued gently, 'which are made manifest to children and to those of simple mind, and not to others. This may be one of those things, perhaps.'

He turned towards the door.

'I shall go straight to Henry's,' he said. 'He will know all about white robins, I've no doubt. What an excitement for the village, Miss Read! We are wonderfully blessed.'

His parting smile forgave me, and this particular Doubting Thomas returned to face an uproarious class.

By my desk stood Helen Coggs.

'I told you I sin 'un!' she said reproachfully.

CHAPTER TWO

The Odd Man Out

By the time the news of our rare visitor had gone round the village, Fairacre School had broken up, and I was as free as my pupils to enjoy all the pleasures of summer.

I had a week at home before setting off for a fortnight's holiday with a friend in Yorkshire, and naturally kept an eye open for the white robin during that time. But I was unlucky.

Birds in plenty visited the bird table, including robins. At this stage of the year most of them looked harassed and shabby. All the hours of daylight were spent in flying to and fro in a ceaseless search for food for their clamouring babies.

On one occasion only did I see a baby robin, paler than its agitated father certainly, but nowhere near being albino. It emerged from the box hedge in my garden, its mottled breast gleaming in the sunlight, its wings trembling with anxiety for food. Snatching some crumbs from the bird table, the adult robin bustled back to the bold child which had followed him, and appeared to hustle it away into the protection of the hedge. I saw it no more.

I ventured quietly several times into the weedy haunt where the albino robin had been seen, and scratched my legs on the vicious brambles abounding there as I strained to see over the mossy wall into the vicarage garden. But again, I was unlucky.

The day before I was due to go away, I walked along the village street to the Post Office. Just emerging into the sunshine were Henry Mawne and a small boy.

'This is my great-nephew, Simon,' said Henry, introducing us. 'Say "How do you do" to Miss Read.'

'Hello,' said Simon, looking acutely embarrassed.

He was a very fair child with silky, almost white, hair, and startlingly blue eyes. I judged him to be about seven or eight, and definitely underweight.

'Are you staying here long?' I asked him.

He looked anxiously at Henry Mawne.

'Possibly for a fortnight,' Henry answered for him. He began to fish in his pocket and produced a crumpled pound note.

'Hop back and get me a packet of foolscap envelopes from Mr Lamb,' he said to the boy. 'I forgot them when we were in the Post Office.'

The child vanished, and Henry Mawne spoke rapidly.

'He's my nephew's boy, and my godson. Trouble at home at the moment. His poor mother's very highly strung, and has just had another attack. Under hospital treatment at the moment, and my nephew is beside himself. We thought it would be a good thing for everyone concerned to have the boy down here for a time. Difficult for us though. We're too old to have children round us, and he's not an easy child, I must admit. Precocious in some ways, and a baby in others.'

'If he's still with you when I get back,' I said, 'bring him to tea. And if you want some books for him, the schoolhouse shelves are bulging with them.'

'Most kind, most kind! Ah, here he is!'

The child handed over the envelopes and change solemnly.

'Well, enjoy your break, Miss Read. No sign of the robin, I suppose?'

'Not yet. I'm living in hope though.'

We made our farewells, and Simon gave me a dazzling smile on parting.

There was no doubt about it. Simon might be pale and skinny, but he was a very handsome little boy.

I arrived back from my Yorkshire holiday on a fine August afternoon.

Driving south I noticed the farmers busy in the harvest fields, and when I reached home Mr Roberts was already combining the great field which lies beyond my hawthorn hedge.

The air was filled with the clatter and throb of machinery as the monster skirted my boundary, and then faded to a constant thrumming as it chugged into the distance.

Mrs Pringle, the school cleaner, was in my kitchen. She 'puts me straight', as she terms it, once a week, and despite her glum disposition which at times infuriates me, I welcome her ministrations, if not her comments, on my abode.

'Had a good time?' she enquired.

'Perfect!'

'Some people are lucky! I could do with a break myself, but a chance'd be a fine thing.'

'I'll put on the kettle,' I said diplomatically, 'I'm sure you need a cup of tea, and I certainly do.'

'It wouldn't come amiss,' she agreed, wringing out

a wet duster. She sounded somewhat mollified, and her next remark sounded positively enthusiastic.

'You missed something this afternoon.'

'What was that?'

It was obviously something pleasant from the clear satisfaction she showed in the fact that I had missed it.

'That funny robin! He come to the bird table not half an hour ago.'

'Really? How marvellous! You *were* lucky to see him. I haven't yet.'

Mrs Pringle tucked her chins against her throat with every appearance of pleasure.

'Well, I was always one for noticing things, and I'd put out the crumbs from your bread bin which you'd forgotten to scrub out before leaving. Seems he liked them, stale though they were.'

'What's he like?' I said, ignoring the slur on my slatternly ways. In any case, I am used to Mrs Pringle's comments on my housewifery.

Her normally dour countenance lit up.

'Oh, he's a pretty dear! He was perched on the table with

the sun behind him, and he looked just like a fluffy snowball. Except for his red breast, of course. He's a real beauty, I can tell you!'

'Let's hope he comes back soon,' I said, making the tea. 'I believe robins like biscuit crumbs. And mealworms. But I don't think I can face handling those.'

'I'll get old Mr Potts, as lives next door to me, to bring up some. He uses 'em for fishing. Come to that, I could bring up some in a jar when I come up to scrub the school out.'

'Don't you mind messing about with maggots?'

Mrs Pringle stirred her tea briskly.

'I'd do *anything* for that robin,' she declared stoutly.

If Mrs Pringle felt such devotion, I thought, what must be the rest of Fairacre's reaction to our rare bird?

'Who else has seen it while I've been away?'

'Ah now, let me think!' Mrs Pringle put her cup down upon the saucer with much deliberation. Her mouth was pursed in concentration.

'There was Mrs Partridge,' she said at last. 'And Mr Willet who was hoeing the vicar's rosebed last week. He was dumbstruck, he told me. Said he'd seen a white blackbird over at Springbourne when he was a lad, but never a white robin! Of course, he didn't see it real *close*. Not like I did just now.'

Mrs Pringle looked smug.

'Anyone else? Any of the children? I hope they won't scare it.'

'Not as I've heard. But Mr Mawne has built a funny little house in the vicar's garden, all covered in branches and that, with a few spy holes to look out of. Got his camera in there, so they say.'

'A hide,' I said.

'No, his *camera*,' repeated Mrs Pringle.

I let it pass.

'He's going to write a bit for the *Caxley Chronicle* and wants a picture to go with it. He's a clever one, that Mr Mawne.'

'He is indeed. I hope he manages to get a photograph.'

'Well, if he does, I reckon we'll get plenty more wanting to take snaps of our robin. Bring plenty of visitors to Fairacre, that bird will, I shouldn't wonder.'

'I hope not,' I said. 'I'm beginning to think that the less said about it the better. We don't want strangers frightening it away.'

Mrs Pringle's neck began to flush and her four chins to wobble. I know the signs well. Mrs Pringle had taken umbrage.

'You asked me yourself to tell you about the bird,' she began. 'We can't expect to keep a thing like that secret, so it's no good getting hoity-toity about it.'

'Sorry, sorry!' I cried. 'You misunderstood me. Have another cup of tea.'

Mrs Pringle buttoned up her mouth and pushed her cup towards me. The gesture was conciliatory, but I could see that I was not forgiven.

*

Certainly the advent of this little albino robin was causing a surprising stir in Fairacre.

For instance, the village fête, usually held in the vicarage grounds on a Saturday in August, was shifted this year to the garden of Henry Mawne at the other end of Fairacre.

There was considerable discussion about this locally.

'It's Mr Mawne's doing,' said one inhabitant accusingly. 'Just because he's bird-barmy us has to keep out of the vicar's garden. All for a *bird*!'

Others defended the plan.

'It's the right thing to do!'

'This white bird's *special*. No point in frightening it off. Why, it might go to Beech Green! And who'd want that?'

'Anyway, it'll make a nice change to go to the Mawnes, and Mrs Mawne's doing the teas herself.'

'Bribery,' muttered the first speaker, but it was plain that she was in the minority. Ninety per cent of Fairacre's population were devotedly in favour of giving the white robin every chance of survival.

Henry Mawne called one morning to return a book he had borrowed. We sat on the garden seat and I begged to be told the latest news.

'As far as I can tell there are four young robins. The other three are of normal colouring.'

'And where is the nest?'

'Oh, without doubt, in the ivy on the wall! This brood will be the last this season, I'm sure. It really is most exciting! I have seen the albino about half a dozen times now, and have taken several snaps which I'm about to develop.'

I told him that Mrs Pringle had seen it, and also that I rather feared that the bird was too popular for its own safety.

He nodded thoughtfully.

'Firstly, it's the children who might frighten it,' he said at last, 'but I'm sure you will do all in your power to protect it when they return to school. It faces danger too from other birds, as well as from any madman with a gun.'

I reassured him.

'And how is Simon?' I asked, now that the question of children had cropped up. 'Is he still with you?'

'No, he's returned home. I was going to say, "thank goodness", but that sounds heartless.'

'Children can be exhausting. Even angelic ones.'

'Oh, Simon's no angel, I can assure you! But he's plenty of reason to be difficult.'

He paused for a moment, as if trying to decide whether to confide in me or not. The cat wandered up and began to weave about my legs. I scratched the tabby back near the tail, a ploy most cats enjoy, while the silence lengthened.

'The fact is,' exploded Henry at last, 'the boy is

odd man out in his family! There are three much
older than he is – all sturdy, dark-haired extroverts
like their father, my nephew. Not a nerve in their
bodies! Strong as horses, never ill, good at games,
and work as well. All out in the world and thriving.'

'Much older than Simon then?'

'Yes, he was one of these little afterthoughts, and
I don't know that he was particularly welcome.
Teresa thought her family was off her hands, you
see, and then Simon came along.'

'Is she fair like the little boy? I thought he was a
very handsome child.'

'So's his mother. Yes, a very pretty girl with a mop
of fair hair. You could quite see why David fell for
her.'

He sighed.

'*Very* pretty,' he repeated, 'but quite unsuitable.'

'Why?'

'A bundle of nerves. Always imagining she has
something the matter with her. The complete hypo-
chondriac! You should see their medicine cabinet.
Twice the size of normal, and crammed with dozens
of patent medicines. It's a marvel to me that the
children are as healthy as they are. Even Simon,
who is so like her, is comparatively cheerful, though
no doubt he'll get more morbid as he grows older.'

Henry sounded gloomy.

'There's no reason to suppose that,' I said

comfortingly. 'Apart from being rather thin and pale, he looked pretty healthy to me.'

'He's very attached to his mother, and I don't think it is altogether a good thing. Especially at the moment.'

'Is she too possessive?'

'Far from it. If anything she tends to reject the child. To be honest, I think she resents any attention which is not aimed at herself. My poor nephew is having the hell of a time.'

'Has she seen her doctor?'

'Too often, to my way of thinking, and all he says is something about her age, and being patient, and adjusting to situations, and similar codswallop. Sometimes I wonder if she needs a job of work, something to take her mind off herself. Though I pity anyone who employs her.'

'She certainly sounds most unhappy.'

'So's my poor David! He has to shoulder all the burdens while she sulks in this nursing home.'

'So she is getting treatment?'

'Yes, and at vast expense. They say it's a nervous complaint that should respond to whatever they're doing to her. I only hope it does. David and Simon are having a pretty thin time of it. They have a girl there who keeps house in a sketchy sort of way, but it's all very unsatisfactory.'

He sighed again, and stood up.

'Well, I mustn't burden you with my troubles. Simon took to you, incidentally. You should feel honoured. He doesn't like many people, poor child, and I'm afraid many people don't like him. He has a pretty quick temper, unlike the other three. As I said, he's the odd bird out in that family.'

'Like the albino,' I said to turn his mind to happier things.

At once his face cleared, and he smiled.

'Like the albino,' he agreed. 'What a comfort nature is! Always something there for consolation.'

A sentiment with which I heartily concurred.

The holiday weeks sped by far too rapidly, and I enjoyed myself picking and bottling fruit, making jam, taking geranium cuttings and tidying the garden. I also decorated the kitchen, and although the standard of workmanship was far below that of Mr Willet, our local handyman-sexton-school-caretaker – and general factotum to Fairacre, I was pleased with the result. Even Mrs Pringle commented grudgingly that 'it must be cleaner'.

When people ask me, as they frequently do, what I find to do in the long holidays which form one of the more attractive aspects of my job, I answer with some asperity. I do as they do. I clean my house, attend to the garden, prepare for the winter, go shopping, visit the dentist, put my meagre financial affairs in order, and so on. Why people imagine that teachers fall immediately into a state of suspended animation the minute term ends, I cannot think, but it is an attitude of mind which one often encounters.

As well as my own personal activities during August, I tried to pull my weight socially, helping at the fête in Henry Mawne's garden, supplying a local fund-raiser with a mammoth tray of gingerbread, and dispensing hospitality to a number of friends who had been kind enough to invite me to their homes during the past term. My old friend Amy, who lives at the village of Bent some miles distant, was one of these, and I was surprised to hear that she already knew about our white robin.

'But there's no secret about it, is there?' she enquired. 'You can't keep such a phenomenon to yourselves, you know.'

'I suppose not. It's just that I tremble for the bird. Too much publicity could put it in peril.'

'Rubbish!' said Amy stoutly. 'A sturdy albino robin can stand up to any amount of publicity, I'm sure. Robins are tough birds. I can't see any robin – white or coloured – being pushed around.'

I only hoped she was right, for certainly the subject of our rarity was cropping up quite often in

the course of conversation with friends and neighbours.

What struck me was the affection, one might
almost say reverence, with which they spoke of it.
Country people are not given to sentimentality over
animals. At times I think they go the other way, but I
realize that I am a soft-hearted woman, incapable of
passing a poor flattened hare or a squashed hedge-
hog on the road, without a pang of pity.

Very few of us had yet had a glimpse of the albino
bird, but we eagerly questioned those who had, and
a number of people remembered other white birds of
the past.

On the whole, the blackbirds were those chiefly
recalled, and as Henry Mawne told us that this particular variety of bird made up almost thirty per cent of
albinos, it was not surprising. Miss Clare, who used to
teach the infants at Fairacre School, remembered one
white blackbird who had become very tame and had
enchanted the children of an earlier generation in the
village, and Mrs Willet, who had been one of those
children, also remembered it vividly.

'There's nothing prettier than a pure white bird,'
she declared. 'That one was white as a lily. Made
you think of churches and altar cloths and that,' she
added, waxing poetical.

Was this, I wondered, the reason for the awe

which our white robin was inspiring? Did we unconsciously connect its albinism with holiness and purity? Whatever were the reasons for our interest, there was no doubt that we were all eager to see it, and to cherish it.

*

I was lucky. I did not have to wait long.

On the very last day of the holidays the early sunshine woke me. I sat up in bed, and looked into the branches of an ancient apple tree outside the bedroom window.

There, its tiny talons gripping a lichen-covered twig, sat the white robin. Its eyes were dark and shining against the white satin of its head. The breast was still more orange than red, and glowed against its snowy plumage.

It was a breathtaking sight, and I did not dare to move. For a full half minute it sat there motionless, and then with a flash of white wings, it had gone.

Full of elation, I rose and dressed.

Now I was one of the élite who had actually seen the white robin!

CHAPTER THREE

Snowboy

Term began, and in the usual flurry of settling the new babies in the infant class, and the young juniors in my own, there was little time to give to birdwatching.

Nevertheless, one or two of the children saw the robin, and we all learned a great deal from the long account of albinism in birds generally which Henry Mawne contributed to the *Caxley Chronicle*, complete with photographs taken from his hide in the vicar's garden.

To be honest, the photographs meant more to most of the *Caxley Chronicle*'s readers than Henry's somewhat erudite account of white birds. The early part of Henry's essay was devoted to genetic inheritance which successfully bogged down a number of readers anxious to assimilate the news of the robin rapidly, before passing on to the local football results.

For those still pursuing the subject of albinism there was a tricky passage involving the term NN, standing for the normal robin, and WW standing for the white variety. The offspring, wrote Henry, become NW, and as the albino gene is recessive further complicated combinations and permutations occur. As Mrs Pringle said: 'I didn't take in all that double-north and north-west stuff, but that Mr Mawne must have a good headpiece on him, that's for sure!'

She spoke for most of Fairacre.

As always when something unusual crops up, the subject of white birds occurred in various forms. There was a letter in *The Times* from a north country reader about a white blackbird which frequented his garden. To this Henry Mawne wrote a reply, and all Fairacre basked in the reflected glory when the letter was printed.

At much the same time, whilst I was reading that delightful book *The Country Diary of An Edwardian Lady*, I discovered that one of the January entries mentions 'a very curious Robin' which the author describes as light silvery grey and looking like a white bird with a scarlet breast when in flight. She comments truly, that 'it is a wonder it has not fallen a victim to somebody's gun'.

This fear, of course, was always with us, but we comforted ourselves with the thought that in such a small community as Fairacre we were united in wishing to protect our treasure. Certainly, if anyone were so wicked, or so foolhardy, as to raise a gun against our robin he would bring down the wrath of all upon his head. It would not take long to trace the culprit, that was sure.

That particular September the weather was warm. The low golden rays of the sun glinted upon the bales of straw waiting to be picked up and stacked in the barns. The streams of golden grain which had poured into the waiting wagons were now safely stored.

All the world seemed bathed in golden light. Yellow sunflowers and golden rod in the cottage gardens added to this mellow warmth, and the first few falling leaves gleamed from the ground, awaiting the showers of bronze and gold which would join them later.

The dew was heavy each morning, and the children found mushrooms and early blackberries. In the gardens of Fairacre a bumper crop of plums weighed down the trees: round yellow gage plums dripping with sweetness, the old-fashioned golden drop plums so much prized by the jam-makers and, best of all, the enormous Victorias still awaiting a few days more in the sunshine to reach perfection.

There were plums everywhere. Baskets of plums were carried to neighbours. Bowls of plums stood on kitchen dressers. Bottles of plums gleamed like jewels from kitchen shelves. Jars of plum jam, plum jelly, plum chutney and plum preserves of all kinds jostled each other in kitchen cupboards.

Plums dominated the side desk in the schoolroom where the children left their elevenses. Usually, a few packets of biscuits or crisps, perhaps an apple or a banana, were to be seen but during the plum season the appearance of the ancient long desk was transformed by the local crop, now forming the main item of the dozen or so 'stay-bits', as the old people termed the snacks.

It was a lovely time when Fairacre enjoyed the fruits of its labours. Runner beans were being stuffed into freezers. Great bronze onions hung in ropes from out-house beams, and bunches of drying herbs from kitchen ceilings.

Marrows swayed in nets, like drunken sailors in hammocks. Potatoes rumbled into sacks, and apples were carefully wrapped in quarter sheets of the *Caxley Chronicle* and put to bed in rows in slatted boxes.

Housewives were red-eyed from peeling and pickling shallots, and their fingers appallingly stained by the constant handling of crops.

But who cared? This, for us country dwellers, was the crown of the year. We rejoiced in this plenty, and faced the coming winter with serenity, secure in the knowledge of our squirrels' hoards.

*

Harvest festival, as usual, found our parish church more crowded than at any other service in the year.

Perhaps country people are more conscious of the need for thanksgiving than their town cousins when the crops have been safely gathered in. Certainly the old familiar hymns from *Hymns Ancient and Modern* were sung lustily and sincerely, as our eyes roved over the bounties of the earth displayed in St Patrick's.

The children had contributed to this handiwork, as they had each year for generations. Each pew end bore a bunch of ears of corn, looped by a length of green knitting wool from the needlework cupboard. The base of the font was beautified by a garland of scrubbed carrots alternating with well polished apples. Giant marrows, dark green, pale green, and striped like tigers, were propped up in the porch for all to admire as the worshippers wiped their Sunday shoes on the mat.

The pulpit, the altar, and the steps to the chancel were left to the ladies of the parish to decorate, and a splendid job they made of it. Some said that their efforts were almost too artistic, and that feelings ran high when they were asked to incorporate six large loaves, contributed by the local baker, into their floral scheme.

Mr Partridge, with his usual pastoral tact, managed to calm the ladies' outraged feelings, and the loaves were removed from the delicate arrangements of wild bryony and sprays of bramble to a more suitable setting against the oak of the rood screen where they stood in a sturdy row and were much admired by those in the front pews.

'I very near broke a piece off one of they,' said our oldest shepherd. 'With a bit of tasty cheese that'd have passed the time lovely during parson's sermon.'

But temptation was resisted, and as always, the good things were gathered up after Harvest Festival Sunday and taken to Caxley Cottage Hospital for the patients' delectation.

'When I was there one Michaelmas,' recalled the same old shepherd, 'we had marrer and marrer till it come out of our ears. We was right glad to get back to tinned peas again, I can tell you.'

Mrs Pringle, true to her word, had prevailed upon her neighbour, Mr Potts the fisherman, to provide her with some mealworms for the robin.

She brought them on the first occasion in a round plastic box which had once held margarine.

'There!' she said, whipping off the lid and displaying the revolting wriggling mass under my nose.

'Lovely, ain't they? They should bring the little old boy along.'

She put the open box on the asphalt part of the playground, in full view of the children in the classroom. As the weather was so warm, the door was propped open and there was every chance of someone seeing the robin if it appeared.

Frankly, I was doubtful. It was some weeks since I had enjoyed that breathtaking glimpse, although other robins had come to collect crumbs from my bird table as usual. Nevertheless, the mealworms were duly left in the strategic position selected, and we all waited for results.

We did not have long to wait. A gust of wind tipped over the light container and whipped it towards the school, spreading a trail of squirming maggots in its path.

'It's blown away!'

'It's gorn!'

'Them worms is runnin' away!'

'We've lost 'em!'

'Get 'em quick!'

'You get 'em! I can't touch 'em!'

There was instant pandemonium, and a concerted rush to rescue the mealworms.

'One of you hold the box,' I ordered, 'while the

rest of you collect the worms. I'll go and fetch a heavier box for them.'

I hurried across to my kitchen, secretly thankful to be absent from maggot-collecting, and unearthed an ancient china pot which had once held Gentleman's Relish. It had a fine heavy base and was just deep enough to hold the robins' treat.

The children greeted it with rapture. The maggots were tipped in whilst I averted my gaze, and peace was restored.

There must have been one or two robins watching these proceedings from hiding places in the hedges for within a few minutes a pair came to snatch our largesse. But, to our disappointment, the white one did not appear.

'He'll come one day soon, you'll see,' Mrs Pringle assured the children when they told her of that morning's adventure. 'If I brings them worms regular, you won't have to wait long. You mark my words.'

The Gentleman's Relish jar was approved by the lady, and after that was in daily use.

'If I was you,' said Mrs Pringle, 'I'd have some of these nice maggots on your bird table. After all, that's where I saw him once, and maybe he's too timid to come into the open, seeing he's so conspicuous. You try it, Miss Read.'

Averse though I was to handling the things, I could see the sense of Mrs Pringle's argument, and I was also so eager to woo the robin to our territory that I braced myself to shake a few mealworms on to the bird table each day, shuddering the while.

There was no doubt about it, robins adored them. I only saw one robin at a time actually on the table, although I felt fairly sure that the pair which frequented the jar in the playground both came separately to my garden. I became convinced that they had nested somewhere in one of my hedges and that some of the young robins, now to be seen about, were their offspring.

I had no means of telling if other robins from the vicarage garden also came to get the mealworms from my table, but I suspected that they did. They must have watched very sharply for there were no fights. Any outsiders were careful to come when the coast was clear, so that there were no squabbles over territory, as often happens.

As the weather grew colder, more and more birds sought out the scraps provided, both on my garden bird table, and in the playground. They seemed to come in groups. A blue tit would appear, followed by half a dozen more. Then the chaffinches would sense that here was food to be had, and the blackbirds and always, of course, the ubiquitous sparrows and starlings.

They would make a concerted rush upon the food available, and then something would startle them and the bird table would be empty in a flash of wings. It was after just such a sudden exodus when I was turning away from the window that the white robin came again.

With his matchstick legs askew, and his liquid dark eyes cocked upon the bounty, he was poised there for a full minute pecking at the scraps which he now enjoyed alone. His orange breast glowed like embers against the snowy feathers. He was even more handsome than on his first appearance.

And he was bolder. He must have glimpsed a movement of mine, for he hopped about to face me, head still cocked, but picked up a maggot without undue hurry and flew off with it in the direction of the vicar's garden.

Later, that same day, the children saw him come to the mealworms in the playground, select a fine specimen, and depart.

It certainly looked as though Mrs Pringle's prognostications were correct.

By the time term ended, the white robin had become a frequent visitor to both my bird table and the playground, although he always chose to come when there were no other birds about.

He was now affectionately termed Snowboy, Snowball, Snowflake, Whitey, or Robbie by the children, and I had no fears that they would frighten the bird.

They treated it with devotion and deference. For them, and for the majority of Fairacre folk, the coming of this beautiful bird was a little miracle, and when school broke up for the Christmas holidays, I had to promise to cherish 'our Snowboy' on their behalf.

The congregation in St Patrick's Church on Christmas morning was not as large as that which gathered for Harvest Festival, but was certainly bigger than usual.

Many of the housewives were at home supervising the Christmas dinner, but there was a fair sprinkling of visitors to engage our attention, and plenty of new gloves and scarves to admire which had obviously been acquired that morning.

The flowers and evergreens caught our eye. Christmas roses, late chrysanthemums, trails of shiny ivy leaves, holly and mistletoe wreathed the font and pulpit, and two splendid poinsettias flanked the altar.

What with all this excitement, and the thought of presents at home and the feasting to come, it was hardly surprising that the choirboys went a trifle flat. Mr Annett, as organist, thumped out the Christmas hymns in as staccato a manner as was humanly possible, in an effort to quicken the pace, but he might just as well have spared himself.

Fairacre boys, as I know to my cost, 'will not be druv', and they lagged half a bar behind and were blissfully unaware of their choirmaster's rising blood pressure.

I was interested to see my young friend Simon again, standing in the Mawnes' pew and flanked by his dark-haired father, whom I knew slightly, and a pretty fair-haired woman who was obviously Teresa, his mother.

She was tall and slim, wrapped in a short chinchilla coat. She did not join in the singing, but stared straight ahead, ignoring the sidelong glances which both Henry Mawne and her husband David occasionally cast in her direction.

The party came out of church fairly quickly, so that I was able to observe Simon's mother as she came up the aisle.

She was exceptionally pretty, but her face was pale and expressionless. It was the brilliance of her eyes which struck me. They were large and of that intense pale blue which is sometimes seen in fanatics. Garibaldi, they say, had just such eyes, and so too have several unbalanced criminals.

I felt a quiver of fear as my gaze met hers for one fleeting moment. Here, I was sure, was someone desperately unhappy, and potentially dangerous too.

Poor woman! Poor David! But most of all, poor young Simon, I thought, watching his fair head, level with the beautiful grey fur coat, as he followed his mother into the winter sunshine.

CHAPTER FOUR

Bitter Weather

The worst of the winter weather came, as usual, after Christmas. Heavy snow towards the end of January kept a few of the children at home for a day or two, and those that did arrive frequently had coughs or head colds.

So many of the mothers were out at work that I sometimes wondered if a few of the children were sent off to school when they would have been better off at home in the early stages of a cold. In former times, there would probably have been a granny sitting by the fire, or a single aunt who would have been free, and more than willing to care for a sickly child, until its mother came home, but grannies and single aunts also went to work these days, and children had to learn to stand on their own feet rather earlier than my own generation did.

All that I could do was to ensure that the stoves were kept banked up, although there was considerable opposition to this, of course, from Mrs Pringle. I heated the children's milk too, for those who could not face a bottle with flakes of ice at the top, and stirred in a spoonful of drinking chocolate from my store cupboard, if they liked it.

At least most of them were warmly clad these days. Even the Coggs children had wellington boots, and some shabby slippers to change into when they arrived. And, while the weather was at its most bitter, I relaxed my stern rule about everyone playing outside for the full quarter of an hour at break time, and let them cluster round the tortoise stove for half the appointed time.

Snow always brings out the worst in Mrs Pringle. She looks upon it as a personal enemy, a despoiler of clean floors, a hazard to life and limb, and the unnecessary salt rubbed into the wounds of everyday living.

'It isn't as though I was getting any younger,' she grumbled to me after the children had been buttoned up, gloved and scarved, and sent on their way.

'It's this weather as makes my leg flare up,' she continued. 'I don't say nothing about it in the ordinary way, as well you know, Miss Read.'

This was news to me, but I forebore to comment. Experience has taught me to let Mrs Pringle have her head when she is indulging in personal martyrdom.

'But all this extra work Takes Its Toll, as they say. That lobby needs a good scrub out every evening, and I can't do it. As for sacks, I'm down to my last two. I did ask Mr Roberts if he'd got any to spare, but they're all these useless plastic things these days that don't sop up nothing.'

'We could wipe them,' I suggested.

'*Wipe them*?' boomed Mrs Pringle, turning red in the face. 'What good would that do? Might just as well wipe the floor itself while I was at it!'

'Of course, of course!' I said hastily.

'No, I sometimes wonder if the folk who live abroad aren't best off. Take my cousin's boy. He's in South Africa, and she had a letter last week to say he was sunbathing. *Sunbathing*, mark you! In January!'

'Lucky chap,' I said.

'Well,' said the lady, heaving herself to her feet from the desk top where she had been seated. 'This won't buy the baby a new frock. One thing I know, if I win the pools one day I'll spend the winter in South Africa.'

One good thing about the cold spell was that the birds, including Snowboy, came much more boldly for the food we put out.

Even the rooks came down into the playground for our largesse, and one, bolder than the rest, took to balancing precariously on the bird table, much to the annoyance of the smaller birds.

There was no doubt that the coming of Snowboy-Snowball-Snowflake-etc had created much more interest in birds generally in the village, and when we heard that Henry Mawne had been invited to appear on local television and to show some of his pictures on the albino robin, we were heady with pride.

'Henry will be on soon after six o'clock on Thursday,' the vicar told me, 'and if you would care to come and see him on our set, my wife and I would be delighted.'

As the vicar has a colour television I accepted gratefully.

'Watch out for Thursday soon after six!' shouted Mr Lamb from the Post Office, when he caught sight of me at the post-box on the wall of his abode.

'Don't forget Mr Mawne's on Thursday,' warned Mrs Pringle.

We all reminded each other when we met. It was quite apparent that everyone in Fairacre would be watching on the great day.

The *Caxley Chronicle* carried a reminder to its readers on the front page, and was careful to point out that Henry Mawne was one of its distinguished contributors. Side by side with this pleasurable announcement, was the unwelcome news that the price of this valuable journal would be going up by one penny at the next issue. I felt that the editor and staff could not have chosen a better time to make the announcement. Henry Mawne's fame sugared the pill very nicely.

On Thursday evening, I presented myself at the vicarage, and found several other friends there. With glasses of sherry in our hands, we stared at the screen awaiting Fairacre's great moment.

I must say that Henry looked extremely elegant and unusually tidy in the studio. The make-up department seemed to have smoothed over most of his wrinkles, and given him a healthy flush, although the heat from the lights or general excitement might have accounted for his robust look. He was wearing his best hacking jacket and his National Trust tie, and we all agreed that he was a worthy representative of the village.

But naturally enough, the white robin eclipsed him in splendour. About a dozen slides were shown, for the first time, and we sat entranced at the bird's beauty. Henry had certainly managed to get some superb pictures, and when the allotted ten minutes were over, and the screen filled with an appalling picture of a head-on crash, police cars, and ambulances with doors yawning as stretchers were being inserted, we watched the vicar switch off, with relief, and lived once again our splendid distinction on television.

*

It was the next evening when my old friend Amy drove over from Bent.

Amy and I were at college together many years ago, and although she is married, much travelled, always exquisitely dressed and wealthy, in complete contrast to me, we have a great deal in common, and the bond of friendship grows stronger with the years.

She has a tiresome habit of trying to reform me, and another, equally annoying, of trying to find me a husband. Luckily, as the years go by, the chances of this being accomplished grow slighter, and Amy's efforts are less wholehearted, much to my relief.

'My dear Amy,' I have said to her on many occasions, 'you must know, surely, that some people are the marrying sort and some are not. I'm one of the latter, so do stop beating your head against a brick wall. I am perfectly happy as I am.'

I am not sure that Amy really believes me, but she is gradually coming round to the idea that I do not sob myself to sleep each night because I am unwed.

Of course we discussed the programme. In contrast to all Fairacre's enthusiasm, Amy was somewhat cool.

'Personally, I question that bird being an albino,' she said. 'I always understood that a *pure* albino bird had pink eyes and no colour in its legs and so on.'

'Well, it's albino enough for most of us,' I said stoutly. 'And come to think of it, I believe Henry did say something on that point.'

'Not enough. In a brief programme like that he should have been *much* more precise. I've no doubt that he will get plenty of criticism from true ornithologists.'

'But Henry *is* a true ornithologist!' I cried. 'You really are a carping old horror, Amy!'

She began to laugh.

'And you and the rest of the Fairacre folk are absolutely besotted with that blighted bird! But I readily admit that it's a beauty, and I can't say fairer than that, can I?'

'Have a glass of sherry,' I said, forgiving her. 'And tell me all the latest news.'

'You haven't, by any chance, a drier sherry than that, have you?' enquired Amy, watching me pour out a fine tawny glassful.

'Sorry, no! I won this at the summer fête.'

Amy shuddered.

'It's jolly good. Rather like that raisin wine we used to buy in Cambridge at three and six a bottle in the old days. But if you don't like it you can have Robinson's lemon barley water instead.'

'I'm sure this will be delicious,' said Amy, lying bravely, as she accepted the glass.

'What news of Vanessa?' Amy's attractive niece is a great favourite of mine. Now that she is married and lives in a castle in Scotland, I do not see much of her, but we keep in touch.

'Thriving, I'm glad to say. Both children doing well, and I believe she is already planning for a third.'

'Good heavens! Does she really want *three*?'

'She wants *six*, so she says. Personally, I consider it rather selfish, but of course there's much more room in Scotland, and you could lose six children in that barn of a castle without missing them for a fortnight.'

'Well, all I can say is, I admire her pluck. Of course, young things can plan families so much more easily these days, can't they?'

'You shouldn't know anything about it,' said Amy severely, 'as a respectable spinster.'

'You and Lady Bracknell,' I replied, 'would make a good pair. She didn't believe in tampering with natural ignorance either.'

Amy put down her glass.

'Talking of marriage, would you like to meet our new organist at Bent?'

'I don't mind meeting the new organist, but I warn you that I shan't have marriage in mind.'

'I'm having a little dinner party next week. Do

come. The poor fellow knows no one locally, and is in rather wretched digs. I don't think he gets enough to eat. James said he'd be home, and said you must come, as he is so fond of you.'

'Don't flatter me, Amy dear. Of course, I'll come, and I shall look forward to seeing your attractive husband, and the new organist. What's his name?'

'Unfortunately, it's Horace Umbleditch. Quite tricky to say when one is making introductions. But he's quite a charmer, and has a most elegant figure. James said: "Fatten him up, but don't marry him off!" At times, James is a trifle coarse.'

'James is a sensible man,' I told her. 'More sherry?'

'Do you know, I think I will. It's rather like a blend of good quality cough linctus and elderberry wine. It's growing on me.'

'Well, keep yourself in hand. It's no use becoming addicted to the stuff. This is all I've got.'

I filled her glass again, while Amy enlarged on the guests whom I should meet at the proposed party, and I looked forward even more eagerly to my evening out.

The weather continued to be cold and miserable. Although most of the snow had cleared, there were still white patches under the hedges and on the northerly slopes which the sun did not reach.

'It's waiting for more to come,' said Mr Willet gloomily, surveying the dark corner by the vicar's wall. Here, in the cold shade, slivers of snow lay under the bushes, undisturbed by the children. In this weather they rushed to the nearby lavatories, and back again, at record speed, thankful to regain the shelter of the schoolroom and the comfort of the ancient tortoise stoves.

As usual, Mr Willet was right. I would back his judgement about our weather against any professional weatherman in the country. In the last week of term, the skies grew ominously overcast, and one night the snow fell from ten o'clock until six in the morning. Once again the lanes of Fairacre were white. The fields glistened beneath their blanket of snow, dazzling against the dark clouds above them.

The bare black trees and hedges made the whole scene look like a stark charcoal drawing. It hurt one's eyes to look for long. One craved for a splash of colour to warm the bleak outlook.

'You'd think by March,' said Mr Willet, 'that we'd see a bit of sun. Dear knows what's gone amiss with spring these days! Why, when I was a boy we reckoned to pick primroses and violets in March. Not much chance of that this year.'

He watched me scattering crumbs for the birds.

'Poor things! No weather for the young 'uns. Seen anything of our robin?'

'He comes most days. He's looking marvellous,

and I believe he's made a nest in my garden somewhere.'

'Has he now? You watch out that cat of yours
don't get the young 'uns. Be a bit of all right if they
turned out white, wouldn't it?'

Ernest and Patrick had wandered up and were
listening to our conversation. They took up the
theme with enthusiasm.

'How many eggs do robins lay?'

I offered them what scanty knowledge I had
gleaned from the bird book on my shelf.

'About half a dozen, I think,' I hazarded.

'Then we might get six new white ones!' cried
Patrick. He grabbed at a passing infant who had
just arrived. 'Hear that, fatty? We might get lots
more Snowballs this spring.'

'Run inside,' I said to the children. 'I'm just
coming, and it's far too cold to stay outdoors.'

'Well, I hope the boy's right,' said Mr Willet,
preparing to set off to his home. 'Be a fine thing if
we had a few more white 'uns.'

'I've a feeling it doesn't work that way,' I replied.
'Didn't Mr Mawne's article say something about
missing a generation? I must look it up.'

'If it was that bit about the Ns and Ws, I was fair
flummoxed,' admitted Mr Willet. 'I was out of my
depth after two lines of that, but I do remember
there was a bit of doubt about it.'

'I'll ask Mr Mawne when I see him,' I promised.

'That'll be some time. He's off on one of these cruises. Gone to Crete, I believe, on a boat with a lot of other bird people. He's lecturing them, so Mrs Mawne told me.'

'Has she gone too?'

'No, she said she had quite enough of birds in Fairacre without going overseas to see a lot more.'

'She would have missed this beastly cold spring,' I said.

'Ah well! Maybe it'll all be over before you break up. Think of that! You'll have your deck chair up before the month's out!'

'That'll be the day,' I said, folding my coat more tightly about me.

And picking my way through the slushy play-ground, I went into the school to face my duties.

CHAPTER FIVE

A Nest of Robins

I spent a considerable time getting ready for Amy's dinner party, and wished I had asked her the usual question, 'Long or short skirt?', when I had been invited. As it was, I had left this vital question too late to bother her, and weighed up the pros and cons for the umpteenth time.

In this bitter weather a long skirt could be a great comfort. On the other hand, it was the devil to drive in, and in Amy's well-heated house it might well prove too warm. It must be admitted though, that if one wished to honour one's hostess, a long skirt looked as though one had really made some effort.

But then again, one did not want to appear over-dressed, and it seemed that short skirts were in again for evening occasions. Also I had recently bought a stunning silk shirt-waister which Amy had not yet seen, and I was strongly inclined to put it on. After a good deal of shilly-shallying I decided to wear the latter, and if every other woman was sweeping around in floor length kaftans and black velvet skirts, good luck to them!

One of the comforts of middle age, I find, is the comparative peace of mind which engulfs one when one has finally decided what to put on. When young, one's evening can be ruined by the thought that one's shoes are the wrong colour, or one's hair needs shampooing. Advancing age has its modest compensations.

The night was clear and frosty. Some snow still lay along the edges of the road and covered the sloping banks which faced north. The car's headlights made dark tunnels of the trees ahead on my way to Bent, and there were few wayfarers about in the winter cold.

Amy's house was as warm and welcoming as her greeting. Great mop-headed chrysanthemums graced the hall table, and two bowls of shell-pink Lady Derby hyacinths scented her drawing-room. Mine, needless to say, had hardly put their noses through the fibre.

Horace Umbleditch proved to be an elegant man with dark hair and a gold-rimmed monocle swinging on a black silk cord about his neck. From Amy's description I had expected a somewhat pathetic figure, undernourished and shy, but the new organist, although enviably slim, was obviously fit and distinctly voluble. I could see that he would more than hold his own in the assembled company.

James, Amy's husband, enveloped me in a bear's hug, kissed me on both cheeks, and held me at arm's length to admire my new silk frock. One can quite see why James is so attractive to the opposite sex. I am not very susceptible, but even my elderly spinster's heart melts when I meet James. He looks at you very closely, as though you were the only woman he was waiting to see. I think it is because he is short-sighted, and he is far too vain to wear spectacles, but the result is the same, and very pleasurable it is. Knowing James, I forgive all – and there is plenty to forgive – but I adore him.

There were ten of us at dinner, mostly Bent friends, some of whom I had met before. I was interested to see that short skirts outnumbered long by three to two. The vicar's wife sported a long black one, made of such heavy ribbed silk that I longed to stroke it, and the youngest wife present wore a dashing spotted affair with frills reaching to the ground.

As always, Amy's food was delicious. A creamy fish dish, sizzling in our ten ramekins, was followed by pheasant, then lemon sorbet or apple and blackberry tart, and a superb dessert of black and white grapes, pears and peaches.

'Coffee in the drawing-room,' Amy called to me as

I went upstairs. I always relish Amy's bathroom. It is a symphony of primrose yellow and deep gold. Even the soap echoes the colour scheme, and best of all, the towels intended for visitors' use are clearly labelled GUEST. How often, in less elegantly appointed bathrooms, I have wondered whether to wipe my wet hands on a corner of my hostess's – or possibly host's – towel, or use the foot mat. It is plain sailing if there is one of those little huckaback items, embroidered with a lady in a crinoline standing by some knot-stitch hollyhocks, but distinctly daunting if one is confronted by six equally sized towels shoulder-to-shoulder on the towel rail.

Horace Umbleditch brought my coffee and sat beside me.

'Amy has been telling me about your famous Fairacre robin. I'm particularly interested as I know Henry Mawne's nephew slightly.'

'David?'

'That's right. My sister is a neighbour of theirs, and occasionally sits in for young Simon if they are going out. She had heard about the robin from them, of course.'

'It's a terrific thrill for us. So far the robin has thrived. We're hoping there will be more one day.'

'Simon's much impressed, I gather from my sister. She sees quite a bit of the boy. She trained as a Norland nurse and has a very soft spot for young Simon. His mother has been ill, as no doubt you know.'

I said that I did.

'There's some talk of the boy going to boarding school next September. A good thing, I should think. Teresa gets no better, and it's affecting Simon badly. I know my sister worries a lot about the family.'

'They are lucky to have such an understanding neighbour.'

'Well, it works both ways. They have always been good to Irene on the rare occasions when she has been ill. Thank God we're a hardy family, and don't ail much.'

Amy bore down upon us at this juncture and carried Horace off to talk to the young wife in the spotted skirt. As James took his place, I was well content, but I pondered on this comment on Teresa Mawne as I drove home under a starlit sky, and was considerably disturbed. The memory of that blank, blue, fanatical stare was fresh in my mind, and I trembled for those who lived with it.

It was during the last few days of term that I caught a glimpse of the white robin in my garden. To my joy, he was feeding a normal coloured robin, presumably a female, who was quivering her wings and obviously begging for food.

Was this his mate? Would we soon see some young robins? I put these questions to Henry Mawne as soon as he returned form his tour of Crete.

He was looking remarkably hale, with a splendid suntan which contrasted noticeably with the pinched blue complexions of the rest of us Fairacre folk.

'Almost certainly his mate,' he said. 'And I've no doubt you'll soon hear the young birds somewhere in that hedge of yours. But don't expect any white ones. I told you all about that.'

I hardly liked to say that I had not quite taken in this important fact, but Henry guessed.

'I suppose you, and all those silly children, and everyone else in the village for that matter, expects half a dozen snow-white robins this spring.'

'Well—' I began diffidently.

'I don't know why I bother to explain these simple facts, I really don't. Did you read my article?'

'Yes, I did.'

'I made it quite plain, I thought, that the *children* of an albino would be normal in colouring. It is *just possible* that an albino might occur in the grand-children. And then probably only one in four.'

'Thank you for explaining,' I said humbly.

'So do spread the word, Miss Read, that we shall not see any more white robins this spring.'

'I will. But we might see one, say, next year?'

Henry Mawne looked severe.

'That's looking rather far ahead. Anything might happen to this year's brood. I shouldn't like to say that we should see a white one *next* year even. Too many hazards. Your cat for one.'

This wholly unjustified attack on poor Tibby, not even present to defend himself, quite took my breath away.

Seeing his advantage, Henry walked away briskly before I had time to answer.

Easter fell early in April, and although the weather over that weekend remained overcast and chilly, the wind changed towards the end of the week, and welcome sunshine flooded the countryside.

It was wonderful, after such a long bleak spell, to wake to warmth and gentle breezes. The crocuses burst into bloom. The daffodil buds seemed to shoot an inch higher overnight, and in all the cottage gardens hoeing, raking and digging began with renewed hope.

Joseph Coggs appeared on my doorstep and offered his services as assistant gardener. I gladly accepted.

Mrs Coggs was out at work, I knew. The twins were looked after, somewhat sketchily, by a neighbour

who had children of the same age. The youngest pair were taken with Mrs Coggs to work at the various establishments in the village where she was employed as a daily help.

Joseph was the odd man out, and I was glad to have him safely with me, and to enjoy his company at my lunchtime. He seemed happy to come and make himself useful, and certainly appreciated my

cooking. He was observant, and unusually know-
ledgeable about natural life.

I watched him staring at a worm which was wriggling purposefully towards a damp garden bed. He
accepted a mug of coffee without shifting his gaze.

'Them 'as got eight hearts,' he informed me.

'Really?'

'And you chop 'em in half and they makes two
worms.'

'I hope you're not going to try it.'

'Course not!' He sounded affronted.

'What are you going to do when you grow up,
Joe?'

I thought of his drunken father. Not much of an
example there for a young boy.

'I be goin' to be a gamekeeper. Like my grandpa
was.'

'I think you would be good at that.'

'And you gets a new suit every two years. And real
leather boots. Proper tweed the suit is. My grandpa
told me.'

'And where did he work?'

Joseph looked nonplussed.

'A good way off. For some Lord Somebody. Might
have been Aylesbury or round there. My grandpa
liked him, and this Lord Whoever give him a watch
when he was an old man.'

Joseph is not usually so forthcoming, and I was interested to learn something of his background.

'Snowboy's been in and out the box hedge,' he said, handing over the empty mug. 'Shall us go and look?'

'No, no,' I said hastily. 'We mustn't disturb him. Do you think there's a nest there?'

'I bet she's sitting,' said Joseph, 'and Snowboy's taking in some grub for her. What we got today, miss?'

'Cottage pie, and apple fluff.'

'Smashing!' said my gardener, setting off to hoe with renewed energy.

Apart from a couple of days when I was out visiting, Joseph spent most of the hours of daylight with me. It seemed to suit Mrs Coggs, young Joe and me as well. He was no bother, happy and obedient, and opened my eyes to a number of things in the garden I had missed.

A blackbird had built in the crook of two branches in the hawthorn bush. Joseph spotted the nest in a trice, but was careful, I noticed, not to visit it too often.

'Four eggs,' he told me proudly. 'And down the field bank there's a wren nesting, but she's been too durned clever for me. Can't find it nohow, but I'll lay she've got more'n four.'

I quoted the old verse to him.

> The dove said: 'Coo,
> What shall I do?
> For I have *two*!'
> 'Pooh!' said the wren,
> 'I have *ten*
> And bring them up
> Like gentlemen!'

It appealed to the boy, and I had to repeat it several times until he had it by heart, I made a note to teach it to my class next term.

One morning of bright sunshine, I carried his mug out into the garden, but could not see him anywhere. Then I became aware of a grubby hand beckoning me silently towards the box hedge at the farthest corner of the garden.

I approached warily, and with some feeling of annoyance. The boy had been told explicitly to keep well away from the white robin's possible nest. It would be infuriating if the parent birds were disturbed and deserted the nest.

'She'm off for a minute,' breathed Joseph. He was holding aside a sturdy branch. The boy's face was alight with wonder, and I had not the heart to chide him.

There, on the ground, in a mossy cup, lay five robin's eggs, white as pearls, and freckled with tiny pink spots. It was a sight to catch the breath.

'Cover it again,' I whispered, 'and come away.'

We crept quickly back to the garden seat near the house, and almost immediately a flash of white wings showed that Snowboy was returning to see if all was well with his wife and potential family.

'I wonder how many white 'uns among them five,' said Joseph, clutching his mug.

'None this year,' I said.

'Might be two or three,' continued Joseph, still bemused.

'Mr Mawne said we couldn't expect any white birds this year,' I said patiently.

Joseph took a long drink, wiped his mouth on the back of his hand, and settled back with a sigh.

'Wouldn't it be fine if us got *five*?' he cried, eyes shining.

Against such touching faith I was powerless, and gave up.

CHAPTER SIX

Our New Pupil

Term had begun when Henry Mawne rang me one evening.

He sounded unusually agitated, and so was I when he asked if he could call immediately about a pressing matter.

'Of course,' I said. 'Bring Elizabeth and I'll get some coffee ready. What's it about?'

'Oh, I couldn't possibly tell you on the telephone, and I won't bring my wife, though many thanks for inviting her. And please don't bother with coffee. I find it keeps me awake these nights. I'll be with you in half an hour or less.'

If there is anything I dislike it is suspense. Why on earth couldn't Henry have given me some clue? To say, in a somewhat shocked voice, that the subject was unsuitable for relaying over the telephone system, was to bring to mind the worst excesses known to man. What had Henry discovered in our midst? Murder, mayhem, illegitimacy, fraud, bigamy? My mind ranged over all as I tidied away piles of marking, and took out the dead flowers, which I had intended to remove throughout the evening.

It was too bad of Henry to keep me dangling like this, I thought, even if it were for only half an hour. I recalled the poor young wives in war time who were only told that their husbands were missing, and no further word was given to them, often for months or years. One in particular I remembered, who wailed tragically, saying: 'I'd sooner know Bob was *dead*, than not know *anything*!'

There had been looks of horror and disgust at this *cri de coeur*, but she had my entire sympathy.

By the time I had faced a raving lunatic at large in the village, various fatal accidents, unspecified incurable diseases with which the Mawnes had been afflicted and which involved asking me for advice, a court case against me for maltreating a child – a clear case here of guilty conscience, as I had administered a sharp slap to Patrick's leg when he had attempted to kick one of the infants – and a number of other unpleasant contingencies, the doorbell rang, and I hastened to admit my tormentor.

To my chagrin, he looked remarkably calm and happy, the maddening fellow.

'Do sit down,' I said, trying to appear equally at ease. 'Now how can I help?'

'It's about Simon,' he said, coming with admirable

brevity to the nub of the matter. 'Trouble at home again.'

'I'm sorry to hear it.'

'Teresa's had a pretty frightening attack. David came home to find her tearing up everything she could lay hands on. Flowers, Simon's toys, David's books! Ghastly! The worst of it was that poor Simon couldn't get out of the room, and had to watch it all. David feels sure that she might have attacked the boy if he hadn't arrived in time.'

'So what has happened to her?'

'She's back in the nursing home. I honestly don't know if it's the right place for her, but at least she's safe for the moment, and so are David and Simon. The thing is, we've offered to have the child again, and I wondered if you could possibly admit him to the school for an unspecified period?'

'No bother at all,' I assured him. 'We'd like to have him, and he knows some of the other children. He'll soon settle, I'm sure.'

Henry sighed gustily.

'Well, that's a relief. I promised David that I would speak to you and ring him tonight. How soon can he be admitted?'

'As soon as you like.'

Henry rose, and shook my hand warmly.

'I'm so very grateful. It will be a weight off

David's mind. He's due to go to Holland on a business trip of some importance to the firm, and I hope he can still make it. This will help enormously.'

I accompanied him to the door. He was still profuse in his thanks.

I returned exhausted to the sitting-room, and collapsed upon the newly plumped cushions.

'Tibby,' I said to the cat, 'there's a lot to be said for casting your burdens, as long as you are not on the receiving end.'

Mrs Pringle's temper improved with the weather, I was thankful to note. She was even heard to sing, in a deep lowing contralto, as she washed up the dinner plates.

'Glad to see the back of that cold weather,' she admitted. 'I'm thinking we could just about do without the stoves. Wicked to burn fuel when there's no need.'

'I think we'll see how we go until next week,' I said hastily. 'The wind is still quite sharp.'

'Well, we'll wait and see then,' said Mrs Pringle, with unusual docility. 'But the Office won't like it if we wants more coke this term.'

At that moment, the white robin flew down to the

tin of mealworms, snatched up a beakful and flew off to my garden.

'The babies are hatched,' said Mrs Pringle.

'How d'you know?'

'I heard them.'

'Heard them? When?'

Mrs Pringle looked slightly abashed.

'Last evening. I come up with some fresh tea towels, and you was on the phone, otherwise I'd have knocked. I felt I must have a peep.'

'Oh, Mrs Pringle! And you know how we've threatened the children about frightening them!'

Mrs Pringle drew herself up huffily, and her face resumed its normal expression of dudgeon.

'Well, I never *looked*. Wasn't no need. Just as I was creeping up to the nest, old Snowboy flew in, and I could hear them youngsters twittering. Sweetly pretty it sounded, I can tell you.'

'That's marvellous news,' I cried, relief flooding me. 'I must let Mr Mawne know.'

'You needn't bother. I told him myself as I went back home,' said Mrs Pringle, sweeping out majestically.

How is it that that woman always has the last word?

*

Henry brought Simon to school on the following
Monday morning.

The child looked peaky, with dark smudges under
his eyes, but he seemed glad to be with us, and I put
him to sit next to Ernest, who is a kindly child and
enjoys looking after people and animals.

Henry was profuse in his thanks as I accompanied him into the lobby.

'I'm glad to have him,' I assured him. 'How is his mother?'

'Much the same. Elizabeth is visiting her today, and intends to give her news of Simon, but I doubt if she'll be interested. It's a difficult case. Even the doctors admit that, and heaven alone knows where it will all end.'

'Well, you can do no more than you are doing, and at least you have the comfort of knowing she's in safe hands.'

'That's true, as far as it goes. But is *safety* enough? We all want to see her restored to normal mental health, with the usual maternal feelings, and pleasure in family life. But can this nursing home do that? That's what worries me. Are we any nearer curing mental illnesses than we were when the poor things were carted off to the local Bedlam?'

'Of course we are,' I said stoutly, trying to rally the unhappy man. 'I should think more advances have been made in that field than in any other. I'm sure you'll see progress in a week or two's time.'

Henry Mawne shook his head sadly, and made no reply, but clanked across the door scraper and set off towards home. Watching his departing figure, it occurred to me that my old friend had aged suddenly in the past few months, and I could only hope that Simon's mother would improve rapidly before the strain disrupted her family still further.

CHAPTER SEVEN

A Tragedy

May arrived, serene and sunny. There were no 'rough winds to shake the darling buds', and the late narcissi and tulips stood up straight as soldiers in the sunshine.

The children came to school in summer frocks and tee-shirts. The stoves were empty, and polished to jet black for the summer season. Woe betide anyone dropping pencil parings or toffee papers behind the glossy bars of the fire guard! Mrs Pringle intended her handiwork to remain unsullied for several months. An occasional dusting, or a little light attention with dustpan and soft brush was all that should be needed now that her arch-enemy, the coke, was not in evidence.

There was plenty of activity in my box hedge. Snowboy and his mate flew in and out a hundred times a day, and the twittering grew stronger. We all resisted the temptation to peep, but Henry Mawne had a quick look, pronounced that there were definitely four babies, and that they would be out of the nest within the week.

He did not have time to dally on this occasion as he was expecting a telephone call, but I went with him to the gate, and watched him enter the car.

'Any white ones?' I called.

'Of course not,' said Henry, quite snappily, and it dawned on me that probably everyone in Fairacre asked him the same question, despite his reiteration of the fact that we could not expect any albinos in this year's broods.

At the end of May we had our first view of the babies. They were fluttering after Snowboy in the empty playground, clamouring to be fed. I saw them from the schoolroom window, and debated whether I should let the children know the good news. I decided that I would risk opening the door very gently, so that the class could see the family at a distance.

They were so breathlessly quiet you could have heard the proverbial pin drop. One or two stood up at the back of the room to get a better view, but I was touched by their intent silence and look of wonder on their faces.

After a minute or two, the white robin fluttered away towards my garden, followed by his four

vociferous youngsters. His anxious mate met him halfway, and together they shepherded their family towards their home.

Very gently I closed the door.

'Ain't that *nice*!' said Patrick with immense satisfaction.

There was a chorus of agreement, and then Eileen spoke.

'But no white ones.'

There was a general sigh.

'You'd think there'd be *one*!' said Ernest sadly.

'Well, you know what Mr Mawne told us,' I reminded them. 'We might get some next year.'

'My Uncle Henry,' said Simon, in his high polite voice which contrasted so noticeably with his companions' country burr, 'says he's bloody tired of trying to explain just that.'

We were all so taken aback at his casual use of a swear word that he went unreprimanded.

'Very understandable,' I said at last. 'Now take out your atlases, and turn to map eighteen.'

As the summer term progressed, I observed Simon with considerable interest.

He was certainly gaining strength, and seemed much more at ease, although he remained pale and did not seem to put on weight.

He seemed attached to Ernest, his desk mate, and Ernest obviously looked upon our visitor as his special charge, but the rest of the children did not seem to accept the boy completely. I put it down to inbred country suspicion of anything foreign, and realised that I could do little about it except to see that no antagonism was shown towards him.

In some ways Simon was admired. For one thing, he was always immaculately dressed, and his fair hair beautifully trimmed. Also he was quiet – almost laconic – in his conversations with his fellows. Only once did I see the flash of temper about which Henry Mawne had spoken. Someone knocked over his paint water, by accident, ruining his picture. Simon flew at the child, his eyes blazing, but luckily his victim had retreated rapidly and in good order, and nothing worse ensued.

He was also in some demand when it came to team games, for he had an unerring aim, and as a fielder could knock down a wicket at a considerable distance when we played our rudimentary cricket or rounders in Mr Roberts' field. The vicar had presented the school with a set of deck quoits some years earlier and at Simon's plea these were dug out of the cupboard and used at playtime. The base was set up some distance from the birds' mealworm tin, a chalk line drawn for the competitors, and this game, which had been unused for a long time, now found fresh favour in the summer sunshine.

I was particularly pleased about this, as it kept the

children from the alternative attraction of scaling the coke pile, and also from the dark overgrown corner where a number of young birds were making their first forays.

As for Simon, it gave him an extra chance to shine, and I felt sure that this was an excellent thing to help him back to a normal life. The news from home, I gathered from the Mawnes, was dispiriting. Teresa remained in the nursing home, David struggled along on his own, his wife's treatment was hideously expensive and very little progress towards recovery seemed to have been made.

I felt extremely sorry for all of them. The Mawnes looked exhausted. They were not used to children in the house, and of course they were over anxious about young Simon. It could not have been easy for the child either. The Mawnes' house was full of exquisite furniture and expensive carpets, and a boy, even one as comparatively docile as young Simon, must have been a hazard among their treasures.

He had no other child to play with during the long light evenings. The Mawnes did not seem to think of inviting others as companions, or perhaps they felt that they could not face the responsibility. I wished that some of the parents would ask the child to play with their own, but the fact that Simon was staying at 'the big house' may have made them shy of offering an invitation.

The result was that the boy was definitely lonely. I noticed an odd streak in his character, as the time passed. He was easily made jealous.

If I praised someone's drawing, Simon would thrust his own before me. If I singled out one child to be a monitor, Simon would cast a look of bitter loathing in my direction. It was a difficult situation, and ignoring it was not enough, I felt.

Here was a damaged child who had watched his mad mother destroy his treasures before his eyes. He had been the object of her resentment and hatred. Was it any wonder that he too resented anything which drew praise and attention away from himself?

On the other hand, I could not afford to show favouritism, and justice must be done to my permanent pupils. I was particularly anxious that no resentment towards the newcomer should build up. They were a friendly and tolerant collection of children, but one could not expect them to put up with flashes of bad temper.

One instance had put me on my guard. Patrick had drawn a splendid map of Fairacre, a perfect riot of colour, and his industry had earned it pride of place on the wall. Inexplicably, it was found torn in half on the floor. No one would own up to its damage, and as Patrick seemed quite happy when we had mended it with adhesive tape, the matter was dropped, but I felt pretty sure that this was Simon's doing. I sensed too, that the children suspected him. Although this particular cloud blew over, I could not see many such incidents occurring without some retaliation. I could only hope for calm weather ahead.

We continued to see the robin family about, sometimes in the playground, but more often in my garden at the school house.

One unforgettable moment for me came one summer evening when I was washing up at the kitchen sink, and watching through the window the coming and going of blackbirds, thrushes, greenfinches, and a host of tits. The garden seemed full of activity, when suddenly the white robin appeared and perched on a branch of an old plum tree some yards from the window.

The ancient gnarled bark had exuded a sizeable drop of golden resin, over the last few months, and this was illuminated by the rays of the sunset, glowing like some precious bead of amber.

It exactly matched the colour of the robin's red breast, fiery against the purity of its white feathers.

The two spots of warm ambience were a joy to see, one enhancing the other, until the bird flew off again with a whirring of snowy wings, and only the glowing gum remained to remind me of it.

By July the weather was really hot, and we were all beginning to long for some rain for our parched gardens. The children found the heat trying at mid-day, and I had to shift my desk from under the direct rays of sunshine through the skylight.

The shady corner abutting on to the vicar's wall became a popular spot to play, and the deck quoits were shifted into the shady part of the playground. Quite a number of the children elected to take a book under the trees which border the field next to the school during their dinner hour, for the unusual heat did not encourage them to race about in their normal fashion.

Simon, with his fair colouring, seemed to feel the heat more than most of his companions, and moved restlessly about in his desk, sighing at intervals.

One brilliant morning of exceptional heat, he was more fidgety than usual. The schoolroom door was propped open to get any air available, and the children had a clear view of the mealworm tin.

Now that the young birds appeared to be capable of looking for their own food, there were fewer visitors to the tin, but the white robin still made occasional trips, and this morning I realised from the sudden cessation of my class's activities and the rapt attention on their faces that he had arrived several times.

When Simon asked to be excused I was glad to let him go. A walk across the playground might make him settle to his work more readily when he returned.

He was gone for some time. In his absence, the robin must have come once more to the tin, for the children's pens remained poised, and their eyes were fixed on the playground.

Suddenly, there was a sharp cry from Ernest and a horrified gasp from the class at large. To my astonishment, the children rose as one man and surged towards the door, with Ernest in the lead. I leapt forward to see what was going on.

There, at the side of the tin, lay the white robin, a deck quoit hard by. In the shade, near the lavatories, stood Simon, another quoit like a bracelet on his arm. He stood absolutely still, white and shaken, but there was a gleam in his blue eyes which, to my mind, showed triumph.

It was Ernest who picked up the robin. He passed it to me, but continued to stroke the beautiful feathers. It was plain that the bird's neck was broken. Its tiny body lay warm and pathetic in the palm of my hand, and the children stood close to me, their faces anguished and their eyes fixed upon their dead friend.

It was Ernest who broke the silence with a most appalling howling noise. The tears burst from his eyes and sobs racked his body.

The sight of Ernest, the biggest, the calmest, the most reliable boy in the school, reduced to such a state seemed to galvanise the rest of them into action. They turned towards Simon and surrounded him before I had time to reach the child.

When I saw their faces, contorted with fury, I realised how a mob bent upon lynching must look.

For one moment, I feared that I had lost control of my children, but pushing between them, still holding the dead bird, I ordered them to go into school.

They hardly heard me at first, so intent were they upon wreaking vengeance, but gradually one or two began to make their way to the schoolroom door. There were tears on most cheeks now, and I looked at Simon.

He was dry eyed, but obviously terror stricken. As I watched him, he took a deep shuddering breath, and slipped to the ground in a dead faint.

At that moment, the infants' teacher appeared, alerted by the fracas.

'Settle them inside,' I begged her, 'and then come and help me with the boy.'

Five minutes later, Simon was lying on my couch

in the school house. The white robin lay motionless on the window sill, its dead red breast aflame in the sunshine.

My assistant had returned to her double duty, and I went to the telephone.

'Henry,' I said when Mr Mawne answered, 'we are in terrible trouble here. Can you come at once?'

CHAPTER EIGHT

Fairacre Mourns

I was extremely sorry to have to add to the Mawnes' worries, and waited for Henry's arrival with considerable agitation.

I had explained briefly on the telephone about the sad event. It was going to hit Henry doubly hard, I was afraid, both on Simon's account and the rare albino robin's.

The boy still lay listlessly on the couch, his small hands folded on his chest. They looked too fragile to have dealt that deadly blow which would soon shatter the joy of Fairacre.

The crunch of tyres on gravel announced Henry's arrival. I went to meet him, lifting the pathetic corpse from the window sill, and putting it into the patch pocket of my cotton frock.

Henry looked even more shaken than young Simon. I took him to the boy's couch. Henry touched the pale hair gently.

'Feeling better?'

The boy shook his head, and his mouth began to

quiver. It might be a good thing, I thought, if the tears of remorse came now. But the child remained dry eyed and silent.

'Come and have a look at the garden,' I said to Henry, 'while Simon's resting.'

I took him out of earshot. We sat on the garden seat, out of Simon's sight, and I withdrew the little corpse from my pocket.

Henry took it in his hands very tenderly. He

seemed considerably closer to weeping than the boy we had left indoors.

'I wouldn't have had this happen for all the tea in China,' he muttered. 'And to think Simon did it! It makes it so much more horrible. Tell me what happened.'

I explained, while Henry nodded thoughtfully.

'He's an uncanny shot,' he said, 'and that allied to his unpredictable temper makes him a dangerous child, I fear.'

He sighed heavily.

'Sometimes I think he's abnormal. Like his poor mother.'

'He's only abnormal in that he's badly hurt just now. He'll grow out of these tantrums. At the moment he craves attention. That accounts for these violent flashes of jealousy – envy of any child who gets more than he does, and envy of any other object, even an innocent robin, if it is admired.'

'You're kind,' said Henry, 'but I'm past comfort at the moment.'

He held out the robin to me.

'I'll put it in the garden shed, and bury it later on,' I said. 'I've no doubt the children will want to know what's happened to it, but I'm sure none of us can face a harrowing bird funeral, which one or two might favour.'

We walked together through the sunlit garden.

'But what's to be done?' asked Henry. 'The boy can't stay at school, obviously. When does term end?'

'In less than two weeks. And I must say, I think you're right about keeping Simon out of the way of the other children. They are an easy-going lot normally, but this has upset them dreadfully, and I wouldn't like to answer for the consequences. Besides, the child needs rest – nursing, one might almost say. If you and Elizabeth can manage it, I should think he would soon recover with you. I take it David can't have him?'

'Impossible at the moment, and Teresa is no better. She gets these destructive moods, I gather, and they are having to treat her with some sort of tranquillisers. She's done a lot of damage to her room.'

He sighed again, and I felt helpless to comfort him. Truth to tell, I was in a state of shock myself, and was doing my best to control involuntary trembling.

'What an unhappy family!' cried Henry. 'Well, we must do what we can. Thank God, the child goes to prep school in September. He needs an entirely fresh start.'

'He can rest here for another hour or two, if you like,' I offered.

'No, no. You have been more than kind, but you have all the other children to see to. It's a sad day for them all. I'll take Simon back in the car, and we'll get him to bed, and call the doctor. I must get in touch with David tonight when he gets home. Poor boy! He has nothing but trouble.'

Simon was still prone on the couch when we entered, but sat up when Henry said they would be going home.

He was still pale, and seemed shaky as he accompanied his uncle to the door.

He said no word until he reached the car. Then he turned and proffered a small hand – the same hand that had killed our dear robin. I took it in mine.

'Thank you for looking after me,' he said politely, and then clambered in beside Henry.

I watched them drive away. Was that the last I should see of poor young Simon, I wondered?

Well, he was in safe hands, I told myself, and there were others to try and comfort now.

I returned to school with a heavy heart.

The news of the robin's death upset the inhabitants of Fairacre far more severely than I had imagined.

Country people are attuned to violent ends among

animals, and can meet these tragedies with stoical calm. But somehow, the white robin had meant more to them than just another garden bird.

I think that the fact that it had created so much interest in the wider world, after Henry's article and the television programme, made the Fairacre folk intensely proud of their rare visitor. Of course they were genuinely fond of the albino – their doting looks and eager enquiries were proof of that – but without Henry's enthusiasm their interest would have been less keen.

How much he meant was brought home to me sharply by seeing, for the first time, tears in Mrs Pringle's normally stony eyes. I felt profoundly shocked. She had ministered to the bird right from the start, zealously bringing the mealworms he so enjoyed, but I had not realised how devoted she had been to him.

The children were inconsolable, and surprisingly mild in their remarks about Simon's part in the tragedy. Had he been present it might have been a different story, and I was glad that he was safely at the Mawnes'. I had not forgotten the ugly scene immediately after the bird's death.

I was relieved too that they did not demand a funeral for the bird, and accepted the fact that I had buried the corpse near the box hedge. But when

Ernest arrived one morning with a somewhat rickety wooden cross bearing the words:

OUR SNOWBOY

and pleaded for it to be erected on the grave, I had not the heart to refuse. If it gave the children some comfort, then why not?

About a week after the sad event, Amy rang up. She too had heard about the albino bird. News travels fast in the country, I know, but I was surprised that it had travelled so far and so quickly.

'I don't know why you should be,' said Amy, when I remarked on it. 'My window cleaner has connections with Fairacre, and he keeps me up to date with the news. What a horrible shock for you all. What happened?'

I told her, my tongue loosened by her unexpected sympathy. Amy had treated our absorbed interest in the bird with some amusement. I think she felt we were somewhat ridiculous, but now that disaster had come she could not have been kinder.

'Heavens! That makes the whole affair much worse. May I tell Irene Umbleditch?'

'Who?' I said, bewildered.

'You know,' said Amy impatiently. 'You met her brother Horace here.'

'Sorry, sorry! The organist, of course. I remember he mentioned a sister who knew Simon.'

'Well, she's staying with her brother at the moment, and he is standing in for your organist next Sunday, and I said I'd drive him over this evening to try the organ. He's picking up the key from Mr Annett at Beech Green as we come through. It's such a lovely evening, I thought Irene might enjoy the drive too. Can we call to see you?'

'Please do. And certainly tell her if you want to. It's no secret, I'm afraid, but the child is being kept well away from everyone until his father can collect him.'

'Best thing to do,' said Amy heartily. 'He'd probably be torn limb from limb if he encountered any of your pupils in the village.'

I was about to protest indignantly at this slight on my children, but Amy cut me short.

'See you later then,' she said, and rang off.

I took to Irene Umbleditch as soon as we met. She was small and plump with soft dark hair. No one could call her pretty, but she had a sweetness of expression, and a low musical voice which made her instantly attractive.

We women were left together when Horace

departed towards the church, and we wandered round the garden enjoying the warm evening air.

Irene stopped by Ernest's lop-sided cross, and looked enquiringly at me.

'Are they still upset?'

'I'm afraid so. Nothing quite so tearful as when it first happened, but they often mention the robin, and I know they have great hopes of another white one some day.'

'And Simon?'

'They hardly mention him.'

'I meant do you see anything of him? I know he's still with his Uncle Henry.'

'Oh, now and again. He doesn't look very happy, but one could never call the child robust.'

She nodded.

'I should very much like to see him. We always got on well when I did a little baby-minding for Teresa and David. Perhaps Horace would let me call while I'm staying with him.'

'Why not see if they are free this evening?' suggested Amy.

'Let's ring up,' I said. 'I expect Simon's still up on a lovely evening like this, and if not you can arrange another meeting.'

Irene looked a little hesitant, but finally agreed, and we went indoors.

'Shall I get the number?' I asked. Since the tragedy, I had become only too familiar with it.

'Please,' said Irene.

Henry answered. He sounded somewhat bewildered.

'Sorry, I can't hear properly. This line's poor. Just a minute while I put on my spectacles. I always hear better when I'm wearing them.'

I waited patiently, listening to various clicks and mutters as the search went on. At last he spoke again.

'Right! Who did you say?'

'Miss Umbleditch wants to speak to you. She's here with me.'

'Miss Umbleditch? Oh, *Irene*! Good, put her on, please.'

I handed over the instrument with some relief, and rejoined Amy in the garden.

'She's a nice woman,' I remarked.

'Very. Must have been much appreciated when she was a nanny.'

'Why? Isn't she one now?'

'I know she's looking for a permanency in the near future, but I gather she gave up when old Mrs Umbleditch became senile, and stayed with her. She died last month, I'm told, so now Irene's free to find another job.'

We sat on the garden seat in companionable silence. The rooks were flying homeward, and far away some sheep bleated. It was all very peaceful. A heavenly smell of roses and pinks wafted around us, and somewhere, far above, a late lark carolled away before going to bed. How lovely to live in Fairacre, I thought, for the umpteenth time! I never wanted to leave it, and with any luck I could be transported the few yards from the school house to the nearby grave-yard with the minimum of fuss.

I was indulging myself with pleasantly melancholy thoughts of a few sorrowing pupils following my coffin, and trying to decide if it should be a spring or autumn occasion (I was jolly well not going to peg out in high summer!), and had already settled for *Ye Holy Angels Bright* as a good rousing hymn, when Irene returned from the telephone.

'I've said I'll walk down immediately,' she said, her eyes were bright. 'I had a word with Simon too. It was lovely to hear him.'

'I'll run you down,' said Amy, overcoming polite protests. 'You don't know where they live.'

'Well, I'll walk back. Horace should be finished within the hour.'

It was settled that we would all meet again for a drink at my house, and I went to get a tray ready while Amy and Irene departed. On the way, I picked up the heavy china Gentleman's Relish jar which had held the mealworms for Snowboy and his friends. I had put it on the window ledge on the day of the tragedy, but it was in a precarious position there, and would be safer put away in the garden cupboard.

Would it ever be used again, I wondered, as I rinsed it under the tap? I did not intend to leave it in the playground. The school bird table, and my own, would provide adequate feeding space, and the white china pot was too poignant a reminder of our lost robin.

A wave of indignation assailed me as the tap ran. That damned boy! Why should we all have been robbed of our lovely bird? And why should the bird itself have been robed of its joy in flight, in exploring the hedges and gardens of Fairacre, and its growing pleasure in its human friends? Really, it struck at the very roots of justice, I told myself crossly.

Ah well, I sighed, replacing the pot on its allotted shelf, it's an unfair world!

The sound of Amy's car returning brought me back to my immediate duties, and I fetched the tray.

*

There was a beautiful sunset as we sipped our drinks.

Horace was enthusiastic about the organ at Fairacre church, but doubtful about the organ blower in the vestry.

'If it was Ernest,' I told him, 'he will be absolutely reliable.'

'No, this one was called Patrick,' said Horace. 'Ernest was having his hair cut, but will be there on Sunday.'

'Then you have nothing to fear,' I assured him.

'And how did you find Simon?' enquired Horace of his sister.

She turned from admiring the sunset, still dazzled by the blaze across the sky.

'Very sweet, but not well at all. As a matter of fact, I may as well tell you now, I've offered to look after him until he starts school in September.'

Her brother looked startled.

'But what about the jobs you were applying for?'

'They can wait,' said his sister calmly.

'I'm sure the Mawnes would be much relieved,' I ventured.

'Oh, nothing's definite yet. David will have to make the decision, of course. I think Mr Mawne will be in touch with him this evening, but that child wants looking after.'

'You're right about that,' I said.

And no one, I thought privately, is better able to do it than Irene Umbleditch.

CHAPTER NINE

A Second Shock

Term ended a day or two after the visit of the Umbleditch pair, and I went away almost immediately.

A favourite aunt of mine lives in Dorset, and I was with her for three weeks, relishing her astringent views on life in general, and trying to keep up with her outstanding physical energy. Although she is in her seventies she gardens, walks and cycles, chattering the while, and is game for a brisk hand of whist or bridge until midnight. My own life at Fairacre seemed a rest cure in contrast.

Things seemed remarkably quiet when I returned and, of course, I knew nothing of the result of Irene Umbleditch's offer to the Mawnes. I did not have to wait long.

One of my first jobs was to go to the post office and the village shop. The morning was young and dewy. Later it would be really hot, I noted with satisfaction, but the freshness of the morning air brought out goose pimples on my bare arms, as I made my way through the village.

Outside the post office Henry Mawne's car was standing, and inside sat Elizabeth. She looked very smart in navy blue with a moiré silk turban to match.

'We're just off to catch the 9.45,' she said, glancing at her watch, 'but I wish Henry would hurry. As usual, we discovered at the last minute that we had about ten pence in the house, so he has just gone to ask Mr Lamb to cash a cheque.'

'You've chosen a nice day for a spree,' I said.

'No spree unfortunately. Far from it, in fact. David rang last night. His wife died suddenly.'

'No! How dreadful!'

'Luckily, Irene is looking after Simon, so that should help.'

At this point, Henry emerged, stuffing notes into his wallet and looking agitated.

'Don't dare stop,' he called, struggling with his seat belt. 'Got to catch the train.'

With a roar they were off to Caxley, and I went into the post office to buy stamps.

Mr Lamb was alone, and looking unusually grave.

'Heard the news, I suppose?'

'Mrs Mawne told me that Teresa Mawne had died.'

'Did she tell you how?'

'Well, no.'

'Threw herself off the roof of that nursing home evidently.'

'Threw herself?' I echoed aghast.

'Mr Mawne said she's been very violent of late. Seems she broke away from her nurse, rushed up to this roof garden place, nipped over the railings and dropped.'

We gazed at each other in shocked silence.

'Best thing really,' said Mr Lamb at last.

'But ghastly for the family.'

'It is now. But won't be in the long run. There was no future for that poor soul anyway. She was bound to come to some violent end. Had it written in her face.'

This was so close to my own private feelings that I could find nothing to say.

'And what can I do for you?' enquired Mr Lamb, resuming his usual brisk manner.

I told him, and watched him tearing out the stamps with his deft careful fingers. How comforting everyday jobs were in times of shock!

We wished each other goodbye, and I continued on my way to the grocer's in more sober mood.

*

I was careful to say nothing about the Mawnes' loss. As far as I knew, only they, Mr Lamb and I had heard about Teresa's death. If suicide were the cause, then the family might well wish the matter to be kept quiet. No doubt young Simon would be kept in the dark about this aspect of the tragedy. He would be hard enough hit, in any case, by the loss of his mother, little though she had contributed to the child's happiness.

But, versed in the ways of village communication, I was not surprised to hear from Mr Willet that Teresa's end was common knowledge in the community. Well, I thought, at least the news wasn't leaked by me.

Mr Willet had offered to take some geranium cuttings for me and 'to bring 'em on at home', for which I was sincerely grateful. He visited me, sharp knife in hand, one afternoon towards the end of the holidays.

'She was a poor tool, that one,' remarked Mr Willet, referring to David's late wife. 'He got caught in a tangle of fair hair when he was young. Not the first neither. Blondes has a way with 'em. Still, it's sad to see her end this way.'

I agreed, watching Mr Willet's horny hand holding the geraniums aside with great delicacy as he searched for suitable cuttings.

'Can't wonder that boy turned out such a var-
mint,' he went on conversationally. 'If I'd have been
there when our robin was killed I'd have given that
boy the biggest larruping of his borns.'

'He fainted as it was,' I protested.

'Ah! And he'd have fainted a damn sight quicker
with me around! What about the other kids? They
were upset enough, in all conscience! I bet they'd
have set about him proper if you hadn't been there.
We hear 'em, my missus and me, still talking about
their Snowboy. It was a cruel wicked thing to do,
and they don't forget it. Come to that, neither do us
old 'uns.'

'We all miss him,' I said, 'but there was no point
in letting the school run riot once the deed was
done.'

'All I can say is, I hope that blessed boy don't show
his face in Fairacre no more. We've seen enough of
that one. I'm sorry about his ma, of course, but that
don't alter what he done. I can't bring meself to
forgive him, that I can't.'

'I thought you were a Christian,' I said.

'Well, I may be. But I'm what they call a militant
one,' replied Mr Willet, snipping energetically.

'Do militant Christians drink tea?' I asked.

Mr Willet smiled.

'Try 'em,' he said.

*

A few evenings later, Amy called in to tell me about an organ recital being given by Horace Umbleditch to raise funds for Bent church.

'It's the roof fund again,' said Amy, accepting a glass of sherry. 'We hover between the roof and the organ at Bent. If it's not one cracking up, it's the other.'

She surveyed her sherry with approval.

'You didn't win this at a fête,' she commented. 'What happened to the cough linctus?'

'You hogged most of that,' I told her. 'I was driven to spending my hard-earned cash on a bottle of Harvey's.'

'Well, you couldn't have done better,' said Amy kindly. 'Have I told you the latest about Horace?'

I hoped she was not going to tell me more about Teresa Mawne. It was time the poor soul was left in peace, I felt.

'What about him?' I said cautiously. Amy had that speculative look in her eye, which I know from experience goes with her match-making efforts.

'He's moving into a house at the school.'

'What school?'

Amy tut-tutted testily.

'The school he works at! Surely you knew he was
the music master at Maytrees?'

'The first I've heard of it.'

'Rubbish! I'm sure I told you *all* about him when
he first came to Bent.'

'Honestly, I had no idea he taught. I just thought
he was the organist at your church.'

'And very fat he'd get on *that* salary,' said Amy. 'Of course he had to have a job somewhere, and I'm sure I told you all about it. You don't listen half the time.'

'Well, I will now,' I said magnanimously. 'Fire away! So he teaches at Maytrees Prep School, and is going to live there.'

'That's right. There wasn't a house available in the grounds when he was appointed, which is why he had to go into those wretched digs. But now the classics man has retired and there's a nice little house free.'

'Good. More sherry?'

'You'd like it there,' said Amy.

'I'm not likely to be asked to visit very often, I imagine.'

Amy sighed.

'I wish you weren't so *prickly*. Here's a very nice young man – well, perhaps not *young*, but quite spry – and I really think he would like to be married—'

'Amy,' I broke in, 'you are nothing but a meddlesome busybody! How do you know he wants to get married? Like me, he's probably perfectly happy as he is. And in any case, there are lots of more suitable candidates for the honour if he is intending matrimony.'

'Hoity-toity!' cried Amy. 'Very well, I promise never to mention marriage again!'

'Thank God!' I replied.

'But you will come and have a drink before the recital?' said Amy, picking up her bag. 'Horace will be there, of course, and our new doctor who is quite devastatingly good looking, and needs *friends*.'

'Thank you, Amy,' I said resignedly.

During the summer, the bird tables had been less used, but at the beginning of September an unusually chilly spell of weather brought some of our friends back, including several young robins.

The children showed their usual interest, and not surprisingly the name of Snowboy cropped up frequently.

They mourned the beautiful bird with genuine sorrow. He had been a rare and exciting visitor. The mere fact that he had been with us for a comparatively short spell made the memory of him doubly dear. The violence of his end made that memory doubly poignant.

As well as remarks about the dead robin, both verbal and written, there were innumerable pictures made, and even one or two poems. I had tried not to encourage too much harping on our lost albino, hoping that the children's natural exuberance would lessen their grief as the weeks went by, but on the other hand, it seemed to give them some comfort to remember him in various ways, and I thought it best to let the subject wear itself out naturally.

The weather helped. September developed into a warm golden period. With the harvest in, the farmers were busy ploughing, with a retinue of gulls and rooks following the lengthening chocolate-brown furrows.

The children played outside day after day, and our nature walks became more frequent. Before long, the winds of autumn and blizzards of winter would keep us confined within the ancient walls of the little school. We might as well get all the fresh air and exercise while we could, I felt.

This halcyon spell pleased Mrs Pringle too. The floors kept cleaner than usual, and the lighting of the tortoise stoves could be postponed, saving work in bringing in coke from the playground to feed the monsters. She became positively mellow, and I wondered privately if she were sickening for something.

She even offered to come and clean the windows of the school house one evening, and told me the Fairacre news as I rewarded her efforts with a cup of strong tea.

After a brief survey of the vicar's recent bout of

indigestion ('Too much lardy cake for his age'), her niece Minnie's indisposition ('Another baby on the way') and the aggravating habits of her immediate neighbour ('Dragged up in the slums of London, so what could you expect?'), she turned to the young slayer of our lamented robin.

'Never could take to that boy,' said Mrs Pringle. 'Sly! Couldn't trust him, I always said. Looked as though butter wouldn't melt in his mouth, and then he done a wicked thing like that.'

'He'd had a pretty raw deal one way and another,' I pointed out.

'So what? I gets tired of people making excuses for other folks' wicked ways. When I was a girl there was Right and Wrong, and you got a good hiding if you Done Wrong, and not much praise if you Done Right! You should've Done Right anyway, was how my ma and pa looked at it!'

'But things aren't quite as simple as that,' I began, but Mrs Pringle ignored me. You might just as well try to dam the River Thames with a matchstick as to stop Mrs Pringle's flow when she is in full spate.

'But nowadays no one Does Wrong, as far as I can make out. Look at that Mrs Coggs as was had up for stealing. What happened to her? "More to be pitied than blamed," everyone said. "Her with her black-guard of a husband and all them kids, and not very bright up top to begin with." Excuses, excuses! It ends up with no one reckoning to pay the price for Doing Wrong. We've got free will, ain't we? What's to stop us choosing Right? I gets proper fed up with all this namby-pamby way of going on.'

I must admit that a great deal of Mrs Pringle's forthright arguments appealed to me, but I did not intend to say so.

'In Simon's case, his poor mother's illness definitely had an effect on him.'

'Maybe. But he's got a good dad, and a grown-up sister and two brothers. They could've helped, I should've thought.'

'I don't think they were at home then,' I said.

'No, they weren't. I taxed Mr Mawne with it one morning when I met him in the street.'

Trust our Mrs Pringle, I thought.

'Them Mawnes are too old to cope with a young boy. I told him so, and he said there wasn't no one else really free. The sister's married and lives in New Zealand, and one boy's in the army and pushed from pillar to post, as you might say, while I forget now where the younger one is. Cambridge, perhaps, or Oxford, or one of those college places where they idle away their time till they're too old to learn anything.'

I let this trenchant criticism of our revered

universities pass without comment. I was still admiring Mrs Pringle's successful attempts to elicit information from her victims.

'Anyway,' continued my informant, struggling to her feet, 'it's a good thing that Miss Umblething-ummy's taken on the child. Them Mawnes were at the end of their tether, and she looks capable of giving that young man a walloping when it's called for. Though no doubt she lets him get away with murder, like the rest of these folk who should know better!'

She gave me a dark look, summing up, without speech this time, her opinion of those in authority, particularly headmistresses, who let sinners go unpunished.

The organ recital took place at the end of September, and I drove to Amy's along lanes already beginning to take on the beauty of early autumn.

Sprays of glossy blackberries arched from the hedges, and the hazel nuts were plumping up. The lime trees were beginning to shed a few lemon-coloured leaves, and the apples were turning from green to rosy ripeness. It was a time of year when nature showed its kindly side, and the knowledge of winter to come could be comfortably shelved.

Amy's garden blazed with dahlias, and the house was beautifully decorated with bowls full of the velvety blossoms. About two dozen people stood about admiring them, drinks in hand, when I arrived, and among them was Irene Umbleditch.

I made my way towards her. Her brother, elegant as ever, was surrounded by a number of friends. It was quite apparent that Horace had soon found his feet, despite Amy's early solicitude on his behalf.

Of course I enquired about Simon.

'He's settled in fairly well at school,' said Irene. 'We took him down about ten days ago, and the matron has been very kind and kept us in the know. She was told about Teresa. It seemed only right, and I must say, she's a wonderfully motherly person, and Simon seems to have taken to her.'

'He's bright enough,' I said. 'Now that he's settled, he should do very well academically.'

I did not intend to mention the robin incident. It was over and done with, as far as I was concerned, but Irene herself brought up the subject.

'It was an appalling thing to happen,' she said, her face very grave. 'The other children must have suffered dreadfully. Do they still talk about it?'

'About the robin, yes. But they don't speak of Simon.'

'I wonder if they still hold it against him?'

I was torn between the truth and sparing this nice woman's feelings.

'Well,' I began, 'I know they bitterly resent what happened, and they hear their parents and other grown ups discussing the affair, of course. But they are pretty good tempered, and I don't think they bear much of a grudge against Simon now, although they did at the time.'

She nodded.

'He won't speak about it. Whether he'd be willing to come and visit Fairacre again, I don't know, but it certainly wouldn't be wise to try it yet.'

I agreed, and asked her what her plans were now that the boy was at school. Her face lit up.

'I'm taking new babies by the month,' she said. 'You know, from birth on for a few weeks. It's just temporary nursing, my favourite age, and I can fit in Simon's Christmas holidays then, and perhaps his Easter one, if he still needs me.'

'I'm sure his father is very grateful,' I hazarded.

'He can do with all the help he can get,' said Irene soberly. 'I don't think many men could have coped with such misery as bravely as he has.'

'Now, you must come and meet Doctor Manning,' said Amy, bustling up. 'In another half an hour we must make our way to the church. I really believe every seat will be taken. It augurs well for the roof fund, doesn't it?'

CHAPTER TEN

The Long Wait Over

Term rolled on. The usual autumn activities enlivened our school progress – harvest festival, the doctor's medical inspection and preparations for Christmas.

The glowing spell of weather broke at last to give several weeks of rough wind and driving rain. The bird tables were well patronised by chaffinches, greenfinches, blue tits, coal tits, marsh tits, and the ubiquitous sparrows and starlings.

The young robins now sported breasts almost as red as their older relatives, and were bold in coming to the table and looking out for any crumbs scattered by the children at playtime.

Since the advent and death of the albino bird the children took more notice of the robins, I thought. The hope of another white one in the spring was kindled anew as the time passed, and explained, in part, the extra cherishing that came the robins' way.

I mentioned this to Henry Mawne one cold

January day when we met at a managers' meeting at the school.

'Well, don't raise their hopes too much,' he advised me. 'The chances are slight, you know. And I wonder if albino robins aren't better forgotten perhaps. A second tragedy would hurt them badly, and as you know, these albinos can get set upon pretty viciously by the normal birds.'

'Snowboy didn't,' I pointed out.

Henry sighed.

'No, I'm afraid he was set upon by the most vicious predator of all. Man has a lot to answer for.'

He looked so sad that I hastened to drop the subject, but bore his warning in mind.

He came back to the school house with me after the meeting, to collect some bird books I had borrowed.

'Simon all right?' I asked.

'Looking fine. We saw them over Christmas, you know. Seems to like his school, and had a cautiously optimistic report. The head's a kindly sort of chap, and knows about the boy's background. In fact, I told him about the robin. Perhaps I shouldn't have done, but he was such a sympathetic listener, I'm afraid I let it out.'

And probably did you a world of good to do so, I thought.

Aloud I said, 'What did he say?'

'Nothing. But he's going to put the boy in charge of the frogspawn, and I bet those tadpoles will be guarded against all comers.'

'He'll enjoy this term then. He's back, I suppose?'

'Yes, David and Irene took him down last week. That girl is an angel. She came in every day to look after things during the holiday, and it's made all the difference to the child. And to David,' he added, as though he had just realised it.

'I liked her enormously,' I said, 'and hope I shall see her again some time.'

'Won't be for a bit,' said Henry. 'She's off to a case at the end of the month, and thoroughly looking forward to it. Seems strange to me. New babies are so *unfinished*, aren't they?'

'No worse than newly hatched birds,' I said. 'They're positively *grisly* without feathers.'

A look which can only be described as maudlin spread over Henry's features.

'They're *perfect*,' he told me, and I did not contradict him.

Excitement began to mount towards the end of term as the nesting season began. I did my best to warn the children against over optimism, with Henry's words in mind, but I was up against fierce hope, and who could be too daunting after all that they had suffered?

We watched the robins in particular, of course. On two occasions we saw a female fluttering her wings and begging for food, while the male bird fed her attentively. We could not be sure if it was the same pair, but rather hoped that there were two couples. It doubled our chances.

The children were not alone in their hopes. Mrs Pringle had no doubt at all that we should have another albino this time.

'Very possibly two or more,' she pronounced, in the hearing of the children, which alarmed me slightly.

'You'd best get out that mealworm dish again,' she told me. 'Might as well do it now. Get 'em used to bringing their babies along.'

Mr Willet was equally positive.

'If it's happened once it'll happen again. Didn't Mr Mawne say so?'

I responded that Henry had warned us not to hope, but my fears were dismissed disdainfully.

Mr Lamb, Mr Partridge, the Misses Waters, the Hales, Miss Quinn, and in fact everyone in Fairacre, it seemed, awaited the arrival of another albino robin with supreme confidence. I trembled for them.

As far as I could make out, the robins were not nesting in my garden this spring. Henry Mawne had *carte blanche* to roam about it whenever he so wished, in his researches, but he agreed that there seemed to be no sign of a robin's nest, though he had discovered two blackbirds', a tit's and two thrushes' abodes.

The vicar's garden, he told me, seemed more promising, and the bosky corner near the lavatories was under his particular surveillance. I told the children about this, and they obligingly hurried from the lavatories and tried to resist the temptation of lingering in their favourite hiding place. Any embryo albino robin in our vicinity was getting every consideration.

In the end, Henry discovered two robins' nests. One was just over the dividing wall among the vicar's neglected weeds. The other at the far end of the vicar's garden towards the churchyard. We waited avidly for further developments.

Obediently I had put the Gentleman's Relish jar back in the playground, in full view of the class. Mrs Pringle kept it supplied with mealworms, and we had a generous number of bird visitors, including robins. Some days I refused to have the door propped open because of the draught, and the children eyed me resentfully on these occasions.

Their anxiety was summed up, I felt, by one brief incident. They were busy painting one afternoon and the room was blissfully quiet.

Patrick looked up from his work.

'What if we don't?' he enquired.

'Don't what?' I replied, connecting his remark with his artistic efforts.

'Get a white 'un,' he enlarged, ignoring his paint brush dripping wet paint.

As one man, the class rounded on this Doubting Thomas within their midst.

' 'Course we'll get one!'

'Maybe two. Mrs Pringle said so!'

'Shut up, you old misery!'

'Us had one before, didn't us? Well then!'

Patrick quailed before the onslaught, and I had to calm the rabble.

Peace was soon restored, but it was a startling display of undaunted hope. Would it be justified?

It was at the beginning of the summer term that the excitement became intense. Three young robins were seen by the mealworm dish being fed by their parents. Handsome though they were, they were welcomed with modified rapture by the children.

Could there be an albino among this brood which

had not yet been seen? Had the second clutch hatched yet? Was there a white robin among it? How soon should we know the worst? Or best?

It was Mrs Partridge, the vicar's wife, who raised our hopes to even more exalted heights. The vicar passed on the news to me in the lobby, shutting the classroom door with some care.

'I should be sorry to raise their hopes falsely,' he assured me, 'but my wife certainly had a glimpse of something white among those deplorable nettles by my compost heap. Of course, we're keeping a sharp watch from the hide. If only Henry were here!'

We all echoed the vicar's heartfelt cry. Everyone in Fairacre had been bitterly disappointed when Henry had been asked, at short notice, to take over another birdwatching expedition, this time to Turkey. Mrs Pringle, in particular, looked upon his departure as downright treachery.

'Should have thought his place was here with our robins,' she said, 'not gadding off to some foreign place where the birds can't understand the Queen's English.'

Her feelings were shared by all in Fairacre, but not so roundly expressed.

I returned to my children, surprised to find that I was trembling with excitement at the vicar's disclosure. Could it be? Could Mrs Partridge really have seen an albino robin? Or was it, as I had first thought on hearing of Helen Coggs's sighting of Snowboy, just a flutter of white paper or a nodding blossom?

The day was fine, and I propped open the door. The mealworms writhed in their unlovely way in the depths of the china pot. A robin came, dived in his beak, and flew off to feed his family.

The children were copying a notice from the blackboard. It was to be taken home, announcing the times of our school Open Days, and they were doing their best to write legibly, so that their parents would have no cause for complaint.

It was Ernest who saw it first, and how right and proper it was that he should be the one whose eye first lighted upon our little miracle.

Quite alone, the white robin stood, legs askew, and dark eyes cocked upon the mealworms. His snowy feathers gleamed in the sunshine, his speckled breast glowing against the shining white satin of his young plumage.

'He's come,' whispered Ernest, standing up. Behind him the rest of the children rose too, the better to see their long-awaited visitor. Their faces were rapt, their eyes as bright as the white robin's.

Without hurry, fearless in his beauty, the white robin selected a mealworm, spread his dazzling wings into two perfect fans, and made off towards the vicar's wall.

Joyous pandemonium broke out in the class room. Children thumped their neighbours. Children hugged each other. Children crowded round my desk, and made enough noise to raise the roof. We might have been at a football match for all the emotional fervour shown.

In the midst of it, Mrs Pringle entered, black oil cloth bag on arm.

'He's come!' they yelled, surging towards her. 'Another white robin! He's come again!'

Solid as the Rock of Gibraltar amidst the waves of children tumbling around her, Mrs Pringle stood unmoved.

Above the hubbub her voice boomed triumphantly.

'Well, what did I tell you?'

Tales From A Village School

Illustrated by Kate Dicker

Christmas Cards For Forty

Now this afternoon we're all going to make a lovely present to take home. People who fidget, Michael, will be standing outside the door and naturally there will be *no* lovely present for them.

Let me see if I can see two nice children to give out the paper. Don't hold your breath, dears, and don't push out your stomachs like that, Anna and Elizabeth.

Don't touch the paper till I tell you. We don't want dirty marks on our Christmas cards, do we?

Yes, Harold, they're going to be Christmas cards. *Don't touch!*

There now! If you hadn't touched it, it wouldn't have fallen down and been trodden on! All put your hands behind your backs, and stop talking!

The fuss!

Everyone ready? Then listen carefully.

Fold your paper over like this and smooth it gently down the crease.

Richard, your hands! Look at that horrid black smear down your card. All show hands!

What on earth have you boys been doing?

Clearing out what drain?

Miss Judd told you to? I'm sure she told you to wash afterwards as well.

Well, anyway, you should have the sense to do so. Don't quibble! Great children of *five*, *six* some of you, and not enough common sense to wash before Art.

Very quickly run and wash.

The rest of you can sing a little song while we wait.

What shall it be? No, John, not that one your daddy taught you. Perhaps some other time. Let's have 'Bingo'.

Very nice. Here come the others. How wet you boys are!

Who threw water over who? Whom? Who?

Well, never mind. Let's get on or these cards won't be ready till *next* Christmas!

That'll do! That'll do! It wasn't as funny as all that.

All quiet!

Now let me see if the fold is by your left hand. *Left* hand, children. The side by the windows, then.

Good! Now don't turn them over or they'll open backwards.

On the front we're going to draw a big fat robin.
You can copy mine from the blackboard.

Watch carefully. See how I use up all my space.
His head nearly touches the top and his feet nearly
touch the bottom.

Who can do a really beautiful robin? Use your
brown crayon and begin.

Run along, Reggie.

All hold up robins. Some are very small. They look
more like gnats.

Of course, Michael, yours would be different.
Where are you going to put his legs? A fat lot of
good it will be to have them on the next page!

Right. Now shade a nice red patch on his breast
like this.

Now inside in the middle we are going to write
'Happy Christmas' and underneath 'from' and then
your own name.

I shall put 'from Mary'
on the board but you will
put 'from John', or 'Pat',
or 'Michael', won't you,
just *your own name*.
Do you all understand?
Hands up those who
don't understand?

Carry on, then. Beautiful printing. While you are doing that I shall bring you each a piece of red wool to tie round your card in a lovely bow.

Richard, why have you put 'from Mary'? Is your name Mary?

Yes, I know it's on the board, but I explained all that.

Who else has been silly enough to put 'Mary'?

Nearly all of you! Now we shall just have to do them all over again! Another afternoon wasted, and we've got carols to learn, and the school concert tomorrow, and our class party to get ready, and Parents' Afternoon and all the reports to do before the end of the week!

Ah, well! Is that the bell? Lead out to play.

Richard and Joan, collect the Christmas cards and put them all in the wastepaper basket.

The Craftsman

'Seems a pity, really,' said Ernest reflectively, paintbrush poised above his Christmas card, 'All this work, just for one day.'

'You should've chosen a quick way to make 'em,' advised Patrick, beside him. He was experimenting with his first cut-out Christmas tree, a dashing affair, contrived from folded green paper. Ernest watched his neighbour's scissors making dramatic slashes in the paper, little triangles falling like confetti on to

the desk, and he sighed enviously as Patrick opened
out his successful tree.

'Done!' said Patrick smugly, and he applied a pink
tongue to the gummed back of his tree. Ernest
watched him place it carefully in the centre of his
Christmas card. He thumped it with a grubby fist
and leant back to admire the finished article.

'I shall cut out a bird, and stick him on just there!'
He placed a dreadfully bitten fingernail in the corner. 'Then that's finished! Ten I wants altogether,
counting my aunties.'

'Reckon I'll be lucky to get this one done today,'
replied Ernest gloomily, bending to his task. 'Have
to make some at home, I suppose, that's all. Threepence they wants at Mobbs's for cards! Think of
that . . . *threepence*!'

'Ah! But they've got sparkle-stuff on 'em,' argued
Patrick reasonably. 'That always makes 'em a bit
pricey, sparkle-stuff do!' He counted nine pieces of
green paper, stacked them neatly on top of each
other, and started to fold them over. 'See, Ern? This
way I'll get the lot cut out all at once. Bet I gets my
ten done before your one! Old-fashioned, all that
slow ol' painting,' he added scornfully.

Around them, the rest of the class drew and
painted, folded and snipped. They had chosen their
own means of making their Christmas cards, and it

was interesting to see how their choice had varied. Most of the younger ones had chosen to decorate theirs with cut-outs of bright paper. Bulky, scarlet Father Christmases leant at alarming angles, awaiting white trimmings and black boots to their ensembles. Stocky reindeer tended to overflow the available space, leaving room for only midget sledges; and robins, balancing on the pin-point of their claws, like top-heavy ballerinas, were everywhere to be seen.

Most of the girls had preferred to use coloured crayons, and had taken infinite pains in drawing babies asleep, in cots that were so rickety that one would have thought them incapable of supporting the mammoth sacks that hung at their ends. Golliwogs, teddy bears, dolls, ships, trains and striped trumpets balanced at the mouths of the sacks, defying the laws of gravity in a remarkable manner.

Ernest's choice of pencil and paint brush was consistent with his habitual caution and patience. He had chosen to draw a church, set against an evening sky. Its windows were carefully criss-crossed into diamond panes. The door was grooved, and studded at equal distances with heavy pencil dots. The cross of St George floated from its crenellated tower . . . rather stiffly, to be sure, as if it had been well starched and was now aloft in a half-gale of unvarying velocity. All this minute work was largely covered when Ernest applied his paint, and had to be picked out afresh with the finest brush that he could find in the cupboard. Had he been alone his work would have given him unadulterated joy, but the sight of Patrick at his mass-production cast a shadow over his own slow-growing effort.

'When you thinks,' he repeated dejectedly, as he waited for his windows to dry, 'that it's all for one day!' It reminded me of Eeyore's sage remarks on the follies and fusses of birthdays . . . 'Here today, and gone tomorrow!'

'Never mind, Ernest,' I said, trying to cheer him, 'most preparations are just for one day. Getting ready is all part of the fun.' But such sententious nonsense clearly gave Ernest small comfort, and his mouth turned down glumly as he tested the church windows with a delicate fingertip. They had dried to such a fierce orange that one might be forgiven for imagining the entire contents of the building on fire, with pews, cassocks and congregation being done to a turn inside.

Doggedly, Ernest dipped his finest paint brush into the black puddle in his box, and, with his mouth puckered, began the slow, detailed work of picking out the submerged diamond panes. Beside him

Patrick gave a sudden yelp of dismay. He gazed, in horror, from one hand to the other. In each he held the fringed fragments of half-Christmas trees.

'Blow!' said the mass-producer, scarlet in the face. 'I've been and cut through the blessed fold!'

With a smile of infinite satisfaction the craftsman beside him bent to his handiwork again.

Carols for Forty

I shall take you myself for singing this afternoon, children, as Miss Twigg is at home with a sore throat.

Can I go and open the piano?

Can I give out the carol books?

Can we sing the new carol Miss Twigg is learning us?

She's learning Miss Green's too, and we're trying to win 'em.

Remind me, all of you, to take yet another lesson on 'Learning-Winning' and 'Teaching-Beating' to-morrow morning. And I don't want bedlam either here or in the hall. I am looking for two con-scientious and light-footed children who can lead this class at a rational pace from here to the hall door. John Todd, we'll see if you can take a little responsibility today. And Anna.

Miss Twigg always lets someone go first and open the piano.

Very well then. Pat, run ahead. Lead on, the rest of you. Don't gallop, John Todd! I might have

guessed! Nor crawl, maddening boy! Just step it out
briskly. Straight in, children, and stand in your usual
places. For pity's sake, Pat, stop crashing the piano
lid. You children seem to think that baby grands
come down in every other shower.

Are we going to have carols?

Breathing exercises first, dear. All breathe in!
Hold it! Out! *Much too much* noise on the 'Out'!

Miss Twigg says that's old-fashioned. She lets us
do paper bags. We blow and blow at pretend bags,
and then we *do* them, with a bang.

Very well. Blow! And again! Bigger still! Now

pop! *One pop*, children, is more than sufficient. Miss Twigg's nerves must be in better shape than mine, I can see. All on the floor, sit. There is no need, Michael Jones, to roll about all over everyone else. Some of you boys make mayhem with a single movement.

Can we have our carols now?

Miss Twigg always lets us boys give out the books.

All hush! What is this squeaking that is going on?

It's our crêpe soles, Miss. Sideways on, Miss, to the floor, Miss.

Then sit still. I shall give the books out from here. Pass them along to the end, child. Brian Bates, don't hold us all up by peering inside each book.

I left a bit of silver paper in mine last week.

We seem to be six books short. Some of you must share. And that doesn't mean a wrenching match, John Todd. You will be left with the nether half of that book if that's the way you handle it. We'll start

with 'Good King Wenceslas' if it's in C. All listen quietly.

Miss Twigg don't play it like that. She always uses two hands.

That will do. Off you go, and anyone scooping 'Fu-oo-el', like a siren, stands by me. Stop a minute. Is someone singing bass?

It's Eric, Miss. He always honks like that.

Well, Eric dear, it isn't that you aren't *trying*, but your voice is rather strong, so sing rather more softly, will you?

Do let's have our new carol, Miss. Number ten.

One of those mid-European ones, I see; and unfortunately in five flats. I think it might be better to practise that a little longer with Miss Twigg.

Miss, there's someone hollering outside.

It's Miss Judd, Miss.

Open the door for her then. Perhaps Miss Judd would like to hear us sing a carol? There is just time for one more.

Please can it be our new one?

Would you like to hear it, Miss Judd? I think it would sound better unaccompanied. When I can see faces and not backs of heads, John Todd, and Michael Jones has stopped that silly giggling, and Brian Bates has pulled his carol book down from the front of his jersey, and Richard Robinson has quite finished looking at his tongue – I will give you the note.

That was lovely. While you were singing, Miss Judd gave me some good news for you. Miss Twigg is much better and will take your next singing lesson. Isn't that wonderful? For all of us.

Snow on Their Boots

A shrivelling east wind had blown for a week, flattening the winter grass and withering the young wallflower plants. It had whipped cruelly under the school door, where the step had been worn away, hollowed by the scraping of children's boots for eighty years.

During the morning, cold rain had lashed the latticed windows. Later sleet had appeared, and now, by half-past two, the snow came racing down, whirling blackly and madly as one looked up at it against the pallid sky, but drifting dreamily, like feathers, as it settled into the puddles in the playground. I decided to send the children home early. This announcement caused such pleasurable stir, such unbridled joy, that one might have thought that confinement in school was on a par with incarceration in the darkest dungeon, with periods of refined torture thrown in.

'Can you all get indoors?' I inquired, when the ecstasy had died down sufficiently for me to make myself heard. 'Is there anyone whose mother is out?'

'Mine's up the farm on Mondays . . . scrubbing out,' said Patrick, 'but us keeps our key in a secret hiding-place, under a flower-pot by the back door, so I can get in all right.'

'Secret hiding-place!' scoffed his neighbour. ' 'Tisn't no secret if you tells us, is it, Miss?'

Patrick flushed at this taunting. 'It don't matter if us all knows . . . not here in the village. It's for strangers like . . . those men as sells notepaper and that, and those old men walking to the workhouse.'

By this time Ernest's hand had gone up. His mother worked in the nearest town.

'I can go to my gran's, with my sister,' he said, his eyes brightening. I knew the cottage well, and could imagine what a snug haven it would be to children on a bleak afternoon like this. The range would be shining like jet, and giving off a delicious smell of hot blacklead, its roaring fire reflected in the plates and covers on the dresser opposite; while, best of all, on the high mantelpiece would be standing the sweet tin, a souvenir of the coronation of King George V and Queen Mary, rattling with 'Winter Mixture', red and white striped clove balls, square paregoric lozenges and lovely, glutinous mint lumps.

They all trooped into the lobby, and there was a bustle of scarf-tying and glove-finding, and much grunting as wellington boots were tugged on. Away they all straggled, heads bent against the storm; all but one solitary figure, who was rooting about in the corner. It was Patrick.

'Can't find my boots,' he explained.

'See if they are by the stove,' I told him, pulling the pail out from under the sink. The most peculiar things got found here, but today there was nothing but a mammoth spider, which advanced in a menacing manner. I retreated to the schoolroom.

Patrick was running one finger in an aimless way up and down the piano keys. There were no

wellingtons by the fireguard, and his feet were still shod in sandals from which his grey socks protruded, the toes of his sandals having been prudently cut off to allow for growth.

'Are they under your desk?' I persisted. He ambled off and hung upside-down surveying his habitual place and its environs, while I opened cupboards, peered behind the piano and under my own desk. At last we sat down to review the situation. We looked at each other, frowning.

'You can't have come to school in those sandals?'

'Can't've!' agreed Patrick.

'Someone must have gone home in yours by mistake.'

'Must've!' agreed Patrick.

A heavy silence fell. The wall clock ticked and a cinder tinkled into the ash pan. Outside, a flurry of snow hissed against the window.

'Well, Patrick,' I said, at length. 'You can't go home like that, and you can't walk in mine, so what's to be done?'

Patrick's eyes had assumed an intent look. I know it well. Thus does he look during multiplication-table practice, when, having had 'seven eights?' fired at him, he stands, with one leg curled round the other, awaiting inspiration. This time it came.

'In that old play-box,' he began slowly, 'there's a

pair of boots what we used for the *Tin Soldier*. I can get into them.'

We hurried into the infants' room and threw up the heavy lid. Velvet capes, moulting feather boas, wooden swords, paper crowns, beads and fans jostled together; and there, beneath them all, were the boots . . . an incredibly dandified pair of Russian boots with Louis heels. Very dashing they must have been a quarter of a century ago, but they presented a pathetic sight as they stood, side by side, with their tops drooping dejectedly.

Patrick sat on the floor and, with much deliberation, forced his feet in. I hauled him up and we surveyed the effect.

Patrick winced. 'Got my socks rucked up,' he said, and sat down again abruptly. Very slowly he began to  edge them off. Outside, the snow fell faster.

'For pity's sake, Patrick,' I urged, 'hurry up. You'll never be home at this rate!'

I straightened a torn lining, while he smoothed his socks. He put his feet in gingerly and stood up. Then he stamped happily, in the ridiculous things, to get his coat. I gazed anxiously out of the lobby window as he dressed.

'Tell your mother about losing your wellingtons,' I
began, when I became conscious of a certain tension
in the air. Patrick was now fully muffled, and stood
in the porch. His face wore its earlier look of concentration, mingled with some sheepishness.

'Come to think of it,' he said, in a still, small voice,
'I left 'em under the dresser at home, for my dad to
put a puncture patch on.'

'*Patrick!*' I began forcefully but, after one look at

my face, he had prudently withdrawn, and was already battling his way across the playground, in his pantomime boots; preferring, no doubt, the storm that raged outside, to that which was so surely brewing up within.

Forty in the Wings

M iss Judd says we are on in ten minutes, and are
we quite ready?

I hope so, dear. Stand still everyone! If you get so
excited you will forget your words. Holly Elves, stop
sliding up and down in your stockinged feet. This is
no time to get splinters in them. Any wobbly-winged
fairies line up by my desk and I will put a final pin in
you.

Miss, please Miss, you—

For the nineteenth time, Christmas Sprite, *go
away*! You've done nothing but haunt me.

But, Miss, you've never done nothing about them
bells what you said about.

What bells I said about? Stand still, fairy, or I shall
never get these wings straight. Oh, the *bells*! Good
heavens, boy, they should have been sewn on long
ago. Fetch them quickly from the plasticine cupboard.

Do you know, Miss, I can't remember what I have
to say.

Nor can I.

It's funny really, isn't it?

John Todd says he can't remember *nothing at all*. Not even the song part.

Don't panic so, children, it will all come back when you are on the stage. Simply remember to throw your voices right out to 'The Boyhood of Raleigh', and you will do very well.

John Todd says that stage ain't safe and we could easy go through.

'Isn't', not 'ain't', and if John Todd spreads such alarmist rumours I shall have to speak to him.

But, Miss, it does sort of squeak.

Simply the wood moving. You really are the most easily depressed set of fairies I've ever met. No more fuss now. All find a seat before I count three. Fairies, don't keep crashing into each other with those wings. I'm not made of safety pins.

Now when you are quite quiet – *quite quiet* I said, John Todd, fuss-fuss-fuss – I will open the door so that you can hear Miss Twigg's children singing carols.

For mercy's sake, that idiotic fairy in the front, take off those wellingtons! Nobody wants to see fairies galumphing about like a lot of Russians stamping the snow off their boots. Ready now?

Don't they sing lovely!

Very lovely. Lovelily. Beautifully, I mean. They've

only two more carols to sing and then it's our play. Just make sure you've all the things you're supposed to have with you. Mother, where's your wooden spoon for mixing the pudding?

Them babies had it first for Miss Muffet.

Then rush like mad – *creep*, rather – to the babies' room and ask for it back. Hurry now, you are on first.

John Todd says he don't feel very well.

I'm not surprised at all. If I had been making the hideous faces he has behind my back I shouldn't feel very well. All actors feel like this before the play starts. It's nothing to worry about.

I feel funny too.

My legs wobble.

It's my inside that feels the worst. It goes up and then down.

So does mine.

Never mind, never mind, no more complaints now. Let me look at you all and see if you are ready. Father Christmas, where's your beard?

I dunno.

What do you mean, 'You don't know'? You had it just now, didn't you? Where is it? Whatever made you take it off?

Too hot.

Too hot indeed, in the depths of winter too!

Here's a pretty kettle of fish! Everyone search quickly. You as well, Father Christmas, lolling back there sucking your thumb while we slave all round you! The very idea! You are a thoroughly naughty little boy, Brian Bates, and this is the last time you are chosen to act, whether your aunt takes elocution classes or not.

Here it is, Miss, behind the radiator.

Pot black, of course, but you must lump it. Put it on at once and don't dare to take it off again.

Can't breathe.

Brian, understand this. Either you choose to wear that beard cheerfully, or Michael Jones puts on your costume this minute and is Father Christmas instead. Well?

Beard.

I should think so. Now we are all ready. I will open the door just a little. Not a sound!

I can see my mum.

So can I.

Here come Miss Twigg's children. Lead up on to the stage.

It won't really give way, will it, Miss?

Miss, I don't feel well.

Nor me.

Miss, them babies said they never had no wooden spoon off of us, so what had I better do instead of?

Brian Bates says he don't want to be Father Christmas, and he's not going to say his words.

Do we *have* to do this old play?

It's too late to turn back now, children. Fairies, point your toes, all smile! Right, boys, up with the curtain, and hand me the prompt book.